NORTH
CHILLS

Edited by Graeme Hurry

KIMOTA
Publishing

First Published 1994

KIMOTA
Publishing

52 Cadley Causeway,
Fulwood, Preston,
PR2 3RX

paperback ISBN 0-9523439-0-8
hardback ISBN 0-9523439-1-6

Although the places in this book are real, all the characters are entirely fictitious. Any resemblance to any person living or dead is entirely coincidental.

British Library Cataloguing in Publication Data. A catalogue record for this book is available from the British Library.

Printed by Bath Press, Lower Bristol Road, Bath, BA2 3BL

CONTENTS

INTRODUCTION 5
The Storyteller illustrated by Bryan Talbot

ABOVE THE WORLD *Ramsey Campbell* 9
Illustrated by Jim Pitts

DEAD MAN'S HANDLE *Stephen Gallagher* 21
Illustrated by Martin McKenna

GUILTY PARTY *Stephen Laws* 45
Illustrated by Martin McKenna

MACKINTOSH WILLY *Ramsey Campbell* 61
Illustrated by Jim Pitts

WRITER'S CRAMP *David Riley* 77
Illustrated by Jim Pitts

NOTES ON CONTRIBUTORS 95
Illustrated by Martin McKenna and Bryan Talbot

Acknowledgements

The editor is grateful to the following for permission to use copyright material in this book :

Ramsey Campbell for *Above the World*
Copyright © 1979 and *Mackintosh Willy*
Copyright © 1979 by Ramsey Campbell.

Stephen Gallagher for *Dead Man's Handle*
Copyright © 1990 by Stephen Gallagher

Stephen Laws for *Guilty Party*
Copyright © 1988 by Stephen Laws

David Riley for *Writer's Cramp*
Copyright © 1988 by David Riley

and the illustrators :

The Authors and illustrations for *Guilty party* and *Dead Man's Handle*
Copyright © 1994 by Martin McKenna

Illustrations for *Mackintosh Willy, Above the World*
and *Writer's Cramp*
Copyright © 1994 by Jim Pitts

The Storyteller in the Introduction and Notes on Contributors
Copyright © 1994 by Bryan Talbot

This book is dedicated to my mother and father, Alasdair and June Hurry for their support.

INTRODUCTION

The history of the horror story is a confused and debatable subject. Traditionalists usually trace back through written literature to Walpole; however, some more adventurous literary historians look even further back into the pre-literary oral tradition of folk tales. These tales can be traced all over the world but are adapted and changed by the story teller to fit in with local tradition and geography. Local story-tellers were equivalent to TV personalities and shared venues with musicians and dancers in homes and public houses. And the stories varied from moral tales, through foreign adventure to horror.

The evolution of the stories to local areas, especially the ghostly or horrific, gave a personality and poignancy which thrilled far more than stories of far away. This was especially true as many of the stories were told in a 'this-could-be-true' way. A bit like apocryphal (or Urban Myths as they are sometimes called) tales are told today. Who hasn't heard the story of the woman who sued an electrical firm because the instructions for her microwave did not say she couldn't dry her poodle in it? The story told in the light of an open fire by a charismatic story-teller who evoked images in the gloom. Tales of ghosts and monsters haunting local places already shunned by the audience.

So the horror story has its roots firmly embedded in the constantly mutating oral folk tale rather than in the literary tradition, which tried to steer clear of the local crude tales. Walpole and others eventually tapped into this vein, but it was less a start than a change in direction for the horror story.

With the advent of speedy travel, from the horse-drawn carriage onwards, the world has become smaller and the locations for stories, including horror, have become international. This book takes one tiny tottering step backwards to stories set in locations which the authors know well. All the stories are set in the North of England and all the authors are based in the north.

Ramsey Campbell sets many of his stories in real places he has visited or lived in, and this detail lends an uncanny feeling of the reality behind the fantasy of the horrific plot. In the award winning *Mackintosh Willy*, the action takes place in a park in Liverpool. The park exists but the graffiti covered shelter described in the story has long since disappeared. Some say it was the council, but...!

The lakes lend a scenic landscape for Ramsey's *Above The World* story. The Swan Inn and Barf are described in wonderfully accurate detail, but remember, always take Mr. Wainright's little book with you if you ever do visit!

Stephen Gallagher's story, *Dead Man's Handle*, is set in Happymount Park which is in Morecambe, one of the many northern seaside resorts. Glorious in the summer, but deserted and ghostly places in the windswept off-seasons. Happymount Park is almost exactly as Steve describes it - at the moment, but there are plans to turn it into The Mr. Blobby Theme Park in the near future.

Stephen Laws wrote his story, *Guilty Party*, after a bus trip to a Newcastle village for a drinking session. The events are real... up to a point.

Part of *Writer's Cramp*, the story by David Riley, is set in Oswaldtwistle, where David lives and works.

So take a seat and imagine the story told in a northern dialect, in the half light of an old house. Try to imagine that the tales are fiction... try to convince yourself that there is not a terror outside in the dark... waiting.

The Storyteller

ABOVE THE WORLD

by

Ramsey Campbell

Nobody was at Reception when Knox came downstairs. The dinner-gong hung mute in its frame; napkin pyramids guarded dining tables; in the lounge, chairs sat emptily. Nothing moved, except fish in the aquarium, fluorescent gleams amid water that bubbled like lemonade. The visitors' book lay open on the counter. He riffled the pages idly, seeking his previous visit. A Manchester address caught his attention: but the name wasn't his - not any longer. The names were those of his wife and the man.

It took him a moment to realise. They must have been married by then. So the man's name had been Tooley, had it? Knox hadn't cared to know. He was pleased to find that he felt nothing but curiosity. Why had she returned here - for a kind of second honeymoon, to exorcize her memories of him?

When he emerged, it was raining. That ought to wash the fells clean of all but the dedicated walkers; he might be alone up there - no perambulatory radios, no families marking their path with trailing children. Above the hotel mist wandered among the pines, which grew pale and blurred, a spiky frieze of grey, then solidified, regaining their green. High on the scree slope, the Bishop of Barf protruded like a single deformed tooth.

The sight seemed to halt time, to turn it back. He had never left the Swan Hotel. In a moment Wendy would run out, having had to go back for her camera or her rucksack or something. 'I wasn't long, was I? The bus hasn't gone, has it? Oh dear, I'm sorry.' Of course these impressions were nonsense: he'd moved on, developed since his marriage, defined himself more clearly - but it cheered him that his memories were cool, disinterested. Life advanced relentlessly, powered by change. The Bishop shone white only because climbers painted the pinnacle each year, climbing the steep scree with buckets of whitewash from the Swan.

Here came the bus. It would be stuffed with wet campers slow as turtles, their backs burdened with tubular scaffolding and enormous rucksacks. Only once had he suffered such a ride. Had nothing changed? Not the Swan, the local food, the unobtrusive service, the long white seventeenth-century building which had so charmed Wendy. He had a table to himself; if you wanted to be left alone, nobody would bother you. Tonight there would be venison, which he hadn't tasted since his honeymoon. He'd returned determined to enjoy the Swan and the walks, determined not to let memories deny him those pleasures - and he'd found his qualms were groundless.

He strode down the Keswick road. Rain rushed over Bassenthwaite Lake and tapped on the hood of his cagoule. Why did the stone wall ahead seem significant? Had Wendy halted there once, because the wall was singing? 'Oh look, aren't they beautiful.' As he stooped towards the crevice, a cluster of hungry beaks had sprung out of the darkness, gaping. The glimpse had unnerved him: the inexorable growth of life, sprouting everywhere, even in stone. Moss choked the silent crevice now.

Somehow that image set him wondering where Wendy and the man had died. Mist had caught them, high on one or other of the fells; they died of exposure. That much he had heard from a friend of Wendy's, who had grown aloof from him and who had seemed to blame him for entrusting Wendy to an inexperienced climber - as if Knox should have taken care of her even after the marriage! He hadn't asked for details. He'd felt relieved when Wendy had announced that she'd found someone else. Habit, familiarity, and introversion had screened them from each other well before they'd separated.

He was passing a camp in a field. He hadn't slept in a tent since early in his marriage, and then only under protest. Rain slithered down the bright canvas. The muffled voices of a man and a woman paced him from tent to tent. Irrationally, he peered between the tents to glimpse them - but it must be a radio programme. Though the voices sounded intensely engrossed in discussion, he could distinguish not a word. The camp looked deserted. Everyone must be under canvas, or walking.

By the time he reached Braithwaite village, the rain had stopped. Clouds paraded the sky; infrequent gaps let out June sunlight, which touched the heights of the surrounding fells. He made for the café at the foot of the Whinlatter Pass - not because Wendy had loved the little house, its homemade cakes and its shelves of books, but for something to read: he would let chance choose his reading. But the shop was closed. Beside it Coledale Beck pursued its wordless watery monologue.

Should he climb Grisedale Pike? He remembered the view from the summit, of Braithwaite and Keswick the colours of pigeons, white and grey amid the palette of fields. But climbers were toiling upward, towards the intermittent sun. Sometimes the spectacle of plodding walkers, fell boots creaking, sticks shoving at the ground, red faces puffing like trains in distress, made his climb seem a mechanical compulsion, absurd and mindless. Suppose the height was occupied by a class of children, heading like lemmings for the edge?

He'd go back to Barf: that would be lonely - unless one had Mr Wainwright's guidebook, Barf appeared unclimbable. Returning through the village, he passed Braithwaite post office. That had delighted Wendy - a house like all the other small white houses in the row, except for the counter and grille in the front hall, beside the stairs. A postcard came fluttering down the garden path. Was that a stamp on its corner, or a patch of moss? Momentarily he thought he recognized the handwriting - but whose did it resemble? A breeze turned the card like a page. Where a picture might have been there was a covering of moss, which looked vaguely like a blurred view of two figures huddled together. The card slid by him into the gutter, and lodged trembling in a grid, brandishing its message. Impulsively he made a grab for it - but before he could read the writing, the card fell between the bars.

He returned to the road to Thornthwaite. A sheen of sunlight clung to the macadam brows; hedges dripped dazzling silver. The voices still wandered about the deserted campsite, though now they sounded distant and echoing. Though their words remained inaudible, they seemed to be calling a name through the tents.

At Thornthwaite, only the hotel outshone the Bishop. As Knox glanced towards the coaching inn, Wendy appeared in his bedroom window. Of course it was a chambermaid - but the shock reverberated through him, for all at once he realized that he was staying in the room which he had shared with Wendy. Surely the proprietress of the Swan couldn't have intended this; it must be coincidence. Memories surged, disconcertingly vivid - collapsing happily on the bed after a day's walking, making love, not having to wake alone in the early hours. Just now, trudging along the road, he'd thought of going upstairs to rest. Abruptly he decided to spend the afternoon in walking.

Neither the hard road nor the soggy margin of Bassenthwaite Lake tempted him. He'd climb Barf, as he had intended. He didn't need Mr Wainwright's book; he knew the way. Wendy had loved those handwritten guidebooks; she'd loved searching through them for the self-portrait of Mr Wainwright which was always hidden among the hand-drawn views - there he was, in Harris tweed, overlooking Lanthwaite Wood. No, Knox didn't need those books today.

The beginning of the path through Beckstones larch plantation was easy. Soon he was climbing beside Beckstones Gill, his ears full of its intricate liquid clamour as the stream tumbled helplessly downhill, confined in its rocky groove. But the path grew steep. Surely it must have been elsewhere that Wendy had run ahead, mocking his slowness, while he puffed and cursed. By now most of his memories resembled anecdotes he'd overheard or had been told - blurred, lacking important details, sometimes contradictory.

He rested. Around him larches swayed numerous limbs, engrossed in their tethered dance. His breath eased; he ceased to be uncomfortably aware of his pulse. He stumped upward, over the path of scattered slate. On both sides of him, ferns protruded from decay. Their highest leaves were wound into a ball, like green caterpillars on stalks.

A small rockface blocked the path. He had to scramble across to the continuation. Lichen made the roots of trees indistinguishable from the rock. His foot slipped; he slithered, banged his elbow, clutching for handholds. Good Lord, the slope was short, at worst he would turn his ankle, he could still grab hold of rock, in any case someone was coming, he could hear voices vague as the stream's rush that obscured them. At last he was sure he was safe, though at the cost of a bruised hip. He sat and cursed his pounding heart. He didn't care who heard him - but perhaps nobody did, for the owners of the voices never appeared.

He struggled upward. The larches gave way to spruce firs. Fallen trunks, splintered like bone, hindered his progress. How far had he still to climb? He must have laboured half a mile by now; it felt like more. The forest had grown oppressive. Elaborate lichens swelled brittle branches; everywhere he looked, life burgeoned parasitically, consuming the earth and the forest, a constant and ruthless renewal. He was sweating, and the clammy chill of the place failed to cool him.

Silence seized him. He could hear only the restless creaking of trees. For a long time he had been unable to glimpse the Swan; the sky was invisible, too, except in fragments caged by branches. All at once, as he climbed between close banks of mossy earth and rock, he yearned to reach the open. He felt suffocated, as though the omnipresent lichen were thick fog. He forced himself onward, panting harshly.

Pain halted him - pain that transfixed his heart and paralysed his limbs with shock. His head felt swollen, burning, deafened by blood. Beyond that uproar, were there voices? Could he cry for help? But he felt that he might never draw another breath.

As suddenly as it had attacked him, the pain was gone, though he felt as if it had burned a hollow where his heart had been. He slumped against rock. His ears rang as though metal had been clapped over them. Oh God, the doctor had been right; he must take things easy. But if he had to forgo rambling, he would have nothing left that was worthwhile. At last he groped upward out of the dank trough of earth, though he was still light-headed and unsure of his footing. The path felt distant and vague.

He reached the edge of the forest without further mishap. Beyond it, Beckstones Gill rushed over broken stones. The sky was layered with grey clouds. Across the stream, on the rise to the summit, bracken shone amid heather.

He crossed the stream and climbed the path. Below him the heathery slope plunged towards the small valley. A few crumbs of boats floated on Bassenthwaite. A constant quivering ran downhill through the heather; the wind dragged at his cagoule, whose fluttering deafened him. He felt unnervingly vulnerable, at the mercy of the gusts. His face had turned cold as bone. Sheep dodged away from him. Their swiftness made his battle with the air seem ridiculous, frustrating. He had lost all sense of time before he reached the summit - where he halted, entranced. At last his toil had meaning.

The world seemed laid out for him. Light and shadow drifted stately over the fells, which reached towards clouds no vaster than they. Across Bassenthwaite, fells higher than his own were only steps on the ascent to Skiddaw, on whose deceptively gentle outline gleamed patches of snow. A few dots, too distant to have limbs, crept along that ridge. The fells glowed with all the colours of foliage, grass, heather, bracken, except where vast tracts of rock broke through. Drifts of shadow half-absorbed the colours; occasional sunlight renewed them.

The landscape was melting; he had to blink. Was he weeping, or had the wind stung his eyes? He couldn't tell; the vastness had charmed away his sense of himself. He felt calm, absolutely unselfconscious. He watched light advancing through Beckstones Plantation, possessing each successive rank of foliage. When he gazed across the lake again, that sight had transfigured the landscape.

Which lake was that on the horizon? He had never before noticed it. It lay like a fragment of slate, framed by two fells dark as storms - but above it, clouds were opening. Blue sky shone through the tangle of grey; veils of light descended from the ragged gap. The lake began to glow from within, intensely calm. Beyond it fields and trees grew clear, minute and luminous. Yes, he was weeping.

After a while he sat on a rock. Its coldness was indistinguishable from his own stony chill. He must go down shortly. He gazed out for a last view. The fells looked smooth, alluringly gentle; valleys were trickles of rock. He held up his finger for a red bus to crawl along.

Closer to him, red dots were scurrying: ladybirds, condemned to explore the maze of grass-blades, to change course at each intersection. Their mindless urgency dismayed him.

They drew his gaze to the heather. He gazed deep into a tangled clump, at the breathtaking variety of colours, the intricacies of growth. As many must be hidden in each patch of heather: depths empty of meaning, and intended for no eye. All around him plants reproduced shapes endlessly: striving for perfection, or compelled to repeat themselves without end? If his gaze had been microscopic, he would have seen the repetitions of atomic particles, mindlessly clinging and building, possessed by the compulsion of matter to form patterns.

Suddenly it frightened him - he couldn't tell why. He felt unsafe. Perhaps it was the mass of cloud which had closed overhead like a stone lid. The colours of the summit had turned lurid, threatening. He headed back towards the wood. The faces of sheep gleamed like bone - he had never noticed before how they resembled munching skulls. A group of heads, chewing mechanically, glared white against the sky and kept their gaze on him.

He was glad to cross the stream, though he couldn't feel the water. He must hurry down before he grew colder. The hush of the woods embraced him. Had a sheep followed him? No, it was only the cry of a decaying trunk. He slipped quickly down the path, which his feet seemed hardly to touch.

The movement of silver-green lattices caged him. Branches and shadows swayed everywhere, entangled. The tips of some of the firs were luminously new. Wind stalked the depths of the forest, great vague forms on creaking stilts. Scents of growth and decay accompanied him. When he grabbed a branch to make sure of his footing, it broke, scattering flakes of lichen.

Again the forest grew too vivid; the trees seemed victims of the process of growth, sucked dry by lichen which at the same time lent them an elaborate patina of life. Wherever he looked, the forest seemed unbearably intricate. How, among all that, could he glimpse initials? Somehow they had seized his attention before he knew what they were. They were carved on a cracked and wrinkled tree: Wendy's initials and the man's.

Or were they? Perhaps they were only cracks in the bark. Of course she and the man might well have climbed up here - but the more Knox

Above the World

squinted, the less clear the letters seemed. He couldn't recapture the angle at which they had looked unmistakable.

He was still pacing back and forth before the trunk, as though trapped in a ritual, when stealthy movement made him turn. Was it the shifting of grey trees beneath the lowering largely unseen sky? No - it was a cloud or mist, descending swiftly from the summit, through the woods.

He glanced ahead for the path - and, with a shock that seemed to leave him hollow, realized that it was not there. Nor was it visible behind him as far back as the wall of mist. His reluctant fascination with the forest had lured him astray.

He strode back towards the mist, hushing his doubts. Surely the path couldn't be far. But the mist felt thick as icy water, and blinded him. He found himself slithering on decay towards a fall which, though invisible, threatened to be steep. A grab at a crumbled trunk saved him; but when he'd struggled onto safer ground, he could only retreat towards the tree which he had thought was inscribed.

He must press on, outdistancing the mist, and try to head downward. Wasn't there a forest road below, quite close? But whenever he found an easy slope, it would become abruptly dangerous, often blocked by treacherous splintered logs. He was approaching panic. As much as anything, the hollow at the centre of himself dismayed him. He had tended to welcome it when it had grown there, in his marriage and afterwards; it had seemed safe, invulnerable. Now he found he had few inner resources with which to sustain himself.

The mist was only yards away. It had swallowed all the faint sounds of the wood. If he could only hear the stream, or better still a human voice, a vehicle on the forest road - if only he had gone back to the hotel for his whistle and compass - But there was a sound. Something was blundering towards him. Why was he indefinably distressed, rather than heartened?

Perhaps because the mist obscured it as it scuttled down the slope towards him; perhaps because it sounded too small for an adult human being, too swift, too lopsided. He thought of a child stumbling blindly down the decayed slope. But what child would be so voiceless? As it tumbled limping through the mist, Knox suppressed an urge to flee. He saw the object stagger against a misty root, and collapse there. Before he had ventured forward he saw that it was only a rucksack.

Yet he couldn't quite feel relieved. The rucksack was old, discoloured and patched with decay; mist drained it of colour. Where had it come from? Who had abandoned it, and why? It still moved feebly, as though inhabited. Of course there was a wind: the mist was billowing. Nevertheless he preferred not to go closer. The blurred tentative movements of the overgrown sack were unpleasant, somehow.

Still, perhaps the incident was opportune. It had made him glance upward for an explanation. He found none - but he caught sight of a summit against the clouds. It wasn't Barf, for between the confusion of trees he could just distinguish two cairns, set close together. If he could reach them, he ought to be able to see his way more clearly. Was he hearing muffled voices up there? He hoped so, but hadn't time to listen.

He wasn't safe yet. The mist had slowed, but was still pursuing him. The slope above him was too steep to climb. He retreated between the trees, avoiding slippery roots which glistened dull silver, glancing upward constantly for signs of the path. For a while he lost sight of the unknown summit. Only a glimpse of the cairns against the darkening sky mitigated his panic. Were they cairns, or figures sitting together? No, they were the wrong colour for people.

Above him the slope grew steeper. Worse, twilight was setting like mist into the woods. He glared downhill, but the fall was dim and precipitous; there was no sign of a road, only the grey web of innumerable branches. He groped onward, careless of his footing, desperate to glimpse a way. Surely a path must lead to the cairns. But would he reach it before dark? Could he heave himself up the slope now, using trees for handholds? Wait: wasn't that a path ahead, trailing down between the firs? He stumbled forward, afraid to run in case he slipped. He reached out to grab a tree, to lever himself past its trap of roots. But his fingers recoiled - the encrusted glimmering bark looked unnervingly like a face.

He refused to be reminded of anyone. He clung to the hollow within himself and fought off memories. Yet, as he passed close to the next tree, he seemed to glimpse the hint of a face composed of cracks in the bark, and of twilight. His imagination was conspiring with the dimness, that was all - but why, as he grasped a trunk to thrust himself onward, did each patch of lichen seem to suggest a face? The more closely he peered, enraged by his fears, the smaller and more numerous the swarming faces seemed. Were there many different faces, or many versions of a couple? Their expressions, though vague, seemed numerous and disturbing.

For a moment he was sure that he couldn't back away - that he must watch until the light was entirely gone, must glimpse faces yet smaller and clearer and more numerous. Panic hurled him away from the lichen, and sent him scrabbling upward. His fingers dug into decay; ferns writhed and snapped when he grabbed them; the surrounding dimness teemed with faces. He kicked himself footholds, gouged the earth with his heels. He clutched at roots, which flaked, moist and chill. More than once he slithered back into the massing darkness. But his panic refused to be defeated. At last, as twilight merged the forest into an indistinguishable crowd of dimness, he scrambled up a slope that had commenced to be gentle, to the edge of the trees.

As soon as he had done so, his triumph collapsed beneath dismay. Even if he glimpsed a path from the summit, night would engulf it before he could make his way down. The sky was blackening. Against it loomed two hunched forms, heads turned to him. Suddenly joy seized him. He could hear voices - surely the sound was more than the muttering of wind. The two forms were human. They must know their way down, and he could join them.

He scrambled upward. Beyond the trees, the slope grew steep again; but the heather provided easy holds, though his clambering felt almost vertical. The voices had ceased; perhaps they had heard him. But when he glanced up, the figures hadn't moved. A foot higher, and he saw that the faces turned to him were patches of moss; the figures were grey, composed roughly of fragments of slate. They were cairns, after all. It didn't matter: companionship waited at the summit; he'd heard voices, he was sure that he'd heard them, please let him have done so. And indeed, as he struggled up the last yards of the slope, the two grey figures rose with a squeaking and rattling of slate, and advanced heavily towards him.

DEAD MAN'S HANDLE

by

Stephen Gallagher

I can tell you exactly when it happened, because it was late in the summer of 'seventy-four and I was nineteen years old. When I say late I mean sometime around September, getting almost to the end. Why do I remember it so well?

Probably because I've been having bad dreams about it ever since.

It was the year that I got a summer job working for the council, and they sent me to a place down by the seafront called - honest to God, I'm not making this up - Happymount Park. I was the park supervisor's assistant, which meant that I had to help out wherever an extra pair of unskilled hands was needed. The park supervisor was about my father's age and a decent type, which was just as well because I had to have been one of the least able workers that he'd ever been assigned. I hardly knew one end of a wheelbarrow from the other, and my hands were so soft that after that first bruising week I took to wearing heavy work gloves almost all of the time. I don't know what some of the others must have made of me; I'd half-expected resentment, but I think they looked upon me as some kind of a pet or a mascot. I was a student, I always had some impressive-looking Penguin Classic stuck down the side of my lunchbag, I always seemed to know the hardest clues in the *Daily Mirror* crossword. . . and the first time that I sank a shovel into the ground, it stuck there and I had to look for help to get it out again. When I painted railings, I always managed to spatter the asphalt underneath. To keep me out of harm's way I was sent to feed the ducks in the Japanese garden, and two of them actually died.

Personally, I think that was just coincidence.

But by then, my reputation was set.

Most of the other park employees had been hardened by decades of all-weather outdoor work, and seemed to have been knocked together out of tougher material than me - even Vince, and he couldn't have been much older than I was. He already had two years in the Navy, and a set of the most amateurishly-executed forearm tattoos that I'd ever seen. There was him, there was Old Jack, there was Irish Michael who hardly ever spoke and who, when he did, revealed teeth like broken liquorice. Let's face it, the bunch of them could have eaten me alive.

But. . . they didn't.

Only in retrospect can I see how they must have felt. I was so useless, it was reassuring; with hardly a paper qualification amongst them, it must have seemed as if I'd been sent over from the other side of some great intellectual divide to show that the rarified creatures who lived there were actually no great shakes, and nothing to fear. After those near-disasters of the early weeks I found my level, which mostly consisted of general gofering, picking up litter, and changing the dud bulbs in the park's illuminations.

The illuminations. Now, they were what the park was mostly about in the summertime, and they were the feature that drew the evening crowds. Every year the same old canvas and hardboard flats would be trundled out of a council warehouse somewhere, patched and touched-up, and then brought to the park and erected on scaffolding to make larger-than-life nursery rhyme scenes at various points around the gardens. The artwork was kind of homely and unprofessional but the little kids all loved it, even the horrendous attempt at Mickey Mouse that looked like Dustin Hoffman with bats' ears. Copyright? Don't even ask. But set them amidst the greenery and floodlight them at the dying of the day, and even a hardened cynic of nineteen wasn't immune to the magic. If you wanted loud noise and white-knuckle rides, you went to the big amusement park at the far end of the promenade. But if you'd only just learned to walk and talk, and loud noises scared you, and a sure sign of a good time was that you had to be picked up and carried home on somebody's shoulder afterwards, then your parents brought you to Happymount.

It was an old-fashioned kind of a park. I mean, how many of them these days still have deckchairs for rent? Or a special terrace just for the elderly? Or a cafeteria that actually opens every now and again, with ice cream and home-made cakes and not a hint of fast food on the menu? Happymount had them, along with a Crazy Golf course, and a miniature roundabout on a trailer whenever the owner turned up with it, and the Japanese gardens that I already mentioned. They also had a petting zoo at one time, until the goat died. I plead not guilty, I never went anywhere near the damned thing.

And at the far end of the park, on an oval track of maybe five hundred yards or less, ran the Happymount Express.

* * *

Dead Man's Handle

The Happymount Express was one of those miniature trains consisting of a diesel engine and a half-dozen open carriages, the entire thing being scaled for the under-fives. You walked down the main central boulevard of the park and there it was at the end, just before you turned off into the gardens. There was even a little station with a concrete platform, and benches for parents to wait. In the evenings there were coloured lights strung all along the boulevard, and a line of them followed the track out through the woodland right up to the outer perimeter of the park. Beyond that was a fence and then a golf course, a real one this time, but in the evenings this would be in darkness.

The train's driver, ticket-taker, and general maintenance engineer was a man called Len Cunningham. I knew him only as a distant figure, because when he wasn't actually running the train he tended to not to emerge from the long, shanty-style engine shed at the far end of the woodland. The shed opened at both ends and the track ran straight through it, so it doubled as a tunnel. It had been built in a haphazard manner out of wood and corrugated iron, and it looked as if a good fart would blow it all down.

Len Cunningham was middle-aged and overweight. He wore overalls and a railway engineer's cap and he always perched on the back of the tiny diesel engine looking as if he'd rather be somewhere, *anywhere* else. Each ride consisted of three circuits of the track and at the end of each he'd pull into the little station and sit there waiting for the toddlers to disembark and load up. The little ones would fuss around like chickens in a yard, and occasionally some of their parents would be dragged along to squeeze themselves into the carriages as well. They'd look like daytrippers in Lilliput. When everyone was aboard, Len would go along and take the money and give out the tickets, and then he'd walk back up the line to his engine with all the eagerness of a man on the way to his own hanging. Then off around again, going *put-put-put* through the shadows of the trees.

And that was more or less it, all through his working day.

For my part, I liked the evenings best. Not least because there wasn't so much to do. The gardeners all stopped working at five and we tried to get all the rest of the general maintenance done in daylight, so by switching-on time it was usually just me and the boss in our little brew hut that was tucked away in the no-man's land behind the Mad Hatter's Tea Party, killing time until shutdown at nine.

We didn't have much in common, but we seemed to have no problem finding things to talk about.

One night, I asked him about Len Cunningham.

'You don't want to mess with him,' he told me. His name, I remember, was Brian, although everyone called him Big Brian except for Irish Michael, who called him Action Man. He said, 'Len Cunningham is an obstacle course in human relations.'

'I wasn't planning on messing with him,' I said. 'I just wondered what makes him tick, that's all.'

'Fuck knows,' Big Brian said. 'But I'll tell you a story that set up my ideas about him for life.' At this he craned back and took a look through the hut's little window, as if he was getting himself ready for a story with some point to it. This window gave us a narrow angle on the park's main gate, glimpsed through a crisscross of scaffolding and a gap between two of the flats. Big Brian was always on the lookout for what he called 'the yob element', usually local boys of around thirteen or fourteen who'd come in and mess around on the under-fives playground. When he saw them, he'd warn them off. When I did, I'd usually think of a reason for being somewhere else.

And then he said, 'There used to be a kid came in the park about two years ago, Keith I think his name was. He was a big lad but he wasn't very bright, you know what I mean? There could have been something wrong with him. Dropped on his head in the delivery room or something like that, I don't know?

'Retarded?' I said, and he frowned at me not entirely seriously.

'Now, don't get all educated on me,' he said. 'I thought we were getting along fine.'

I made an overly-contrite face. 'Sorry.'

'Anyway, this boy Keith. . . Look what you've done, I've forgotten what the point of the story was, now!'

'I don't know. It was something to do with Len.'

'Right. This boy Keith, he was the kind who used to play with kids half his age. I think *simple* is the word I'm looking for because, you'd look at him and you'd see no harm in him at all. He used to come in the park a lot, and he loved that train. Now if it was me, I'd have taken his money for the first couple of rides and then I'd have looked the other way. I mean, nobody gives a toss, really. But not Len. He took the lad's pennies until he had none left, and then he ordered him off. This was still early in the day, it wasn't even busy. So the next thing is, Len's going around and around on his little train and this lad's running alongside the track, making all the noises. You've seen the speed it goes at.'

We were talking here of a maximum of around eight or nine miles an hour. 'Not exactly hard to keep up with,' I said.

'Well, Len didn't go for this. He didn't like it at all. I was up on a ladder stringing fairylights, and I could see the whole thing. Len's face was starting to look like a bucket of thunder and this lad, he looked as if he was all set to go on following the train around till he dropped. He was getting really giddy and when the train came to a stop, he was jumping around and waving his arms and shouting. So Len got off his little engine and went over to him. He didn't lay a hand on him - I'd have shopped him if he did, I wouldn't have cared if he lost his job for it - but the way he carried on, it made me really sick.'

'What did he say?'

'I can't remember all of it. But it was something like if this boy didn't stop messing around, Len was going to drag him into the tunnel and stick him in an oildrum and boil him down till there was nothing left but bones. Now, you could say that kind of thing to some kids and they'd shrug it off, no problem; they'd know it was a warning and that the rest of it was just, you know. . . '

'Rhetoric?' I offered, but Big Brian had a better word of his own.

'Bollocks,' he said. 'But this Keith, it was like he was on top of the world one second and it was all knocked out of him the next. He just kind of deflated. I couldn't do something like that to anyone. So he's walking away and he's bright red and he's as good as crying, and as he's going past my ladder I call down to him and say, Hey, call him fatso and then run away, he really hates that. So the boy brightens up a bit and looks back and shouts at the top of his voice, *Fat sod! Fat sod!* And then he turns and runs off out of the park.'

'Did he ever come back again?'

'No, but not because of that. He was seen getting into some stranger's car out along the front, one day. The car drove off, and he was never seen again. Made all the papers. Then most people forgot. Next to that kind of behaviour I suppose Len's is just sheer bad manners. But it tells you something about him.'

So, that was Len Cunningham.

Whenever I saw him after that, whether he was walking across the park to his work or perched on the back of his engine like a gorilla on a roller skate, I always thought of him as the Fat Sod. He looked the part and, if Big Brian's story was anything to go by, he'd certainly earned the name.

But I didn't give the matter a lot of thought until about a week later, when I got in one morning to find Big Brian in the brew hut reading a handwritten note. He really needed glasses to read but he wouldn't admit it, and so there was a lot of frowning and peering and holding the note around to find the best light.

Throwing down my lunch bag and picking up the kettle, I said, 'Love letters?'

'You cheeky bugger,' Big Brian said, lowering the note which appeared to have been written on a page torn out of those Challenger account books, the ones with the numbered pages that you can buy cheaply by the dozen on the market. 'Just for that, you can have the job.'

'What job?'

'To put a new lamp in the engine shed for Len. I'm surprised we've lasted this long. He did all his own wiring and they're always burning out.'

'After what you told me last week? No thanks.'

'Go on, stop moaning. He's not even in yet. Take the spare key from the board.'

I'll admit it, I was curious to get a look inside the engine shed as long as I could do it in the absence of the permanent tenant, and this was probably the best opportunity that I was going to get. You know the kind of feeling. It's like getting the chance to read someone else's mail. So I took the key from its hook on the board - I was the first to be using it in ages, if the layer of dust around it was anything to go by - and went around to the next hut to pick up a spare lamp. Then I set out down the boulevard.

The park was almost empty at this hour. I counted about three dog-walkers, one jogger (they were rarer, in those days), and a tramp checking the litter bins for clean newspapers. By the time that I reached the railway tracks, there was nobody at all.

There was a sheen of dew on the grass, making it look as if it had been covered in a fine gauze. I cut across it, through the trees toward the engine shed. There was a chill in the morning, but nothing serious or off-putting. It was the kind of day where you knew that it was going to be fine later on.

Life seemed about as good as it could get, right then.

The engine shed had a kind of hillbilly look about it, considering the way that it had been thrown together out of sheet iron and timber and then patched, shored up, extended and extended again. It was long and low and it had no windows at all. Down at the far end, there was a stovepipe poking up out of the roof. Even that wasn't straight.

I had to walk all the way around, because the nearest of the double-doors was bolted on the inside. Later on when the train was running these would be pinned all the way back to make the tunnel opening, and I could see the arcs scored in the gravel where their lower edges had dragged. Right now the trackbed simply went on under them. It reminded me of those Roadrunner cartoons where the Coyote paints a white line around into a bogus tunnel on a rockface.

There was a big padlock securing the doors at the other end. I had a difficult time opening it, and at one point I thought I was going to have to give up. . . but then I got the angle just right and the key turned easily, and I pulled back one of the doors to go in. The door was in a bad way; a single sheet of corrugated iron, it had dropped on its hinges and screeched loudly as it caught on one of the rails. The iron along the edge was all bent and ripped and rusted, as if this happened every time.

I stepped inside.

* * *

The darkness wasn't total. Anything but. I could see a maze of chinks and needles of light as if I was in a closed barn. I could just about make out the train, filling the shed almost from one end to the other, but otherwise I had to reach around inside the doorway looking for a switchbox so that I could turn on some lights.

I found one. It made some difference, but not much.

I'd never seen in here before. Not in years, anyway, not since I'd have been too small to remember, and then I'd only have been riding through. There was a second spur of track running alongside the main one and connected at either end by a set of points, presumably so that carriages could be run off the main track for servicing and repair. Nothing stood on it now. There was a lot of junk in there; iron, timber, sheet ply, all of it mildewed-looking and stacked against one of the walls. Screened from the track by a makeshift curtain were the stove, a brown table with a teapot, a mug and a half-bottle of rancid milk standing on it, and alongside the stove an oilstained easy chair worn right down to the stuffing in places.

Len's little haven. Further along there was a workbench, and a big drum of diesel oil whose smell was pervading the place. And that wasn't all; because there was also Len's concession to showbusiness.

NORTHERN CHILLS

Whether he'd made it or inherited it, I really couldn't tell. But there was a little tableau in the corner of the engine shed that you'd see from the train as you were leaving the tunnel. I might have been startled by the figure if it hadn't been so patently unlifelike; it was posed like the worst Frankenstein monster ever, with a pick in one hand and a hurricane lamp in the other and a shapeless little hat on its head. It was supposed to be a gold miner. My guess was that it had been made by sticking some thrift shop clothing on a crude frame and then stuffing in some newspaper to give it bulk. The clothing had been daubed with two colours of fluorescent paint, rather like a tar-and-feather job. The figure leaned forward alarmingly, as if the weight of the pick were about to pull it over; at its feet were a heap of gravel, a dirty map with a big X on it, and a few more rusty and broken tools. All that I could see of its face under the hat was a bunch of whiskers that looked suspiciously like the bristles from a yard brush.

And how did I know that it was supposed to be a gold miner? Because there was a handpainted picket sign that said Laredo Gold Mine, jammed at an angle into the tailings pile. I was glad that it was there, because otherwise I would never have known.

'What are you doing in here?' a voice from behind me said.

* * *

I turned around, startled and unaccountably guilty.

Len Cunningham was standing framed in the open doorway. I couldn't see much more than his dark silhouette, but even that was unmistakable.

I swallowed hard.

'I brought the new lamp you asked for,' I said, hoping that my voice would keep steady. 'If you'll show me where it's to go, I can put it in for you.'

He said nothing right away. Just stood there, unreadable.

And then he seemed to decide that, even if he didn't like it, I'd given him an explanation that he couldn't do much other than to accept.

'Just put it on the table,' he said. 'I'll see to it.'

'It wouldn't be any trouble. And it's what I'm here for.'

'I said put it down.'

I put the box down so fast, I almost cracked the glass inside.

Of all the days that he could have come in early, he had to pick this one. Wasn't it just my luck? I stood there fidgeting like a schoolboy in the headmaster's study as he walked past me. Bear in mind that I hadn't been so long out of school, and the habits hadn't yet died. As he lumbered by, I kind of shrank back. I felt like an injured bird being stepped over by a dog, and hoping not to be noticed.

Perhaps he picked some of that up, I don't know. But he glanced back at me, and he seemed to relent a little.

'There's only me knows where everything is,' he said by way of explanation.

'Fine,' I said.

He set his duffel bag down on the table alongside the teapot, took a folded newspaper out of his pocket and dropped it alongside, and then looked at me again.

'Who are you working with?' he said.

And so I told him that I was with Big Brian, and Len snorted with obvious contempt.

'Yeah,' I said, beginning to get some of my nerve back. 'He said you were old mates.'

'Him?' Len said. 'I've got no time for him. He wouldn't give you the pickings from his arse.' And he started to unload the duffel bag. Lunchbox, chocolate, packet of biscuits, a well-worn T-piece of brass which I recognised as the Dead Man's Handle, the speed control without which the train couldn't be run. . .

I needed an exit line, and I didn't have one.

Instead, I heard myself blurt out, 'I wasn't nosing around.'

'There'd be nothing to find if you did,' Len said, and then he pulled out a big handkerchief and blew his nose. The way that he did it, it sounded as if he was shifting about a pint of mucous. He glanced at me over the handkerchief, as if he was beginning to get puzzled as to why I was still here.

'Well?'

'I've got a suggestion,' I said. 'If you get one of those UV tubes and set it on the ground in front of that figure, all that fluorescent paint would glow. They use it in the ghost train down at the other end of the shore. It doesn't cost anything and it's really effective.'

He looked past me, to the tableau behind. But it was only for a second.

'It's only for kids,' he said dismissively.

'We've got spares in the stores. You'd only need the one tube, and you could hide it behind the gravel heap.'

'Nah,' he said, and turned his back.

Which, with nothing further being said, I took as my cue to leave.

* * *

A couple of days later, when Irish Michael and I were brushing away some of the dead leaves and litter that always seemed to pile up in front of Tom, Tom, the Piper's Son - a wind trap, that corner, if ever there was one - Big Brian stopped by and said to me, 'What exactly happened between you and Len the other morning?'

'I told him he was the nicest man I'd ever met,' I said. 'And he spoke very highly of you.'

'You didn't talk about doing up the tunnel?'

'I suggested one of those black light tubes, that's all. The way he's got it now, the lights just show up how cheap and crappy everything is.'

'Well, I wish you'd keep your ideas to yourself. He's asking for all sorts of stuff, here.'

Big Brian handed me another of those torn-off Challenger sheets, and I set down my brush and took a look at it. Irish Michael carried on working, just as if he hadn't seen or heard any interruption. The writing on the paper was spiky and childish, the spelling barely literate; it was the writing of someone to whom penmanship had never been much of a skill even when first learned, and it had rusted unused ever since.

'Yeah,' I conceded, reading down the list. 'Some of this could be my fault.'

'Oh, could it?' Big Brian said. 'Well, when you're finished here you can go and chase all of this stuff down and take it over. Whatever you use, make sure you note it down in the big book. And then the next time you get one of these brilliant ideas, perhaps you'll try keeping quiet about it, eh?'

'Yes, massa,' I said.

If the intention was to make me sorry that I'd opened my mouth, it worked. Len hadn't simply stopped at the thought of a UV tube and a fitting and some cable to wire it in. He wanted more paint, he wanted some timber, he wanted chicken wire, he wanted a tannoy loudspeaker. It took me most of the rest of the day to get it all together, chasing around the various council stores in different parts of the town, and then I had to borrow the gardeners' pickup truck to bring it all back. There was no road out into the woods, but there was a dirt track. Mostly this was used for taking out grass cuttings and dead branches, which were then heaped up and burned in the furthest corner of the park. And I'm pretty sure that Old Jack always waited until the wind direction was right before he had a bonfire day, because he got so much satisfaction out of hearing the golfers choke and splutter as the smoke billowed out across the ninth hole on the adjacent course.

I stopped the truck by the open tunnel, and went around the back to drop the tailgate. The train was working, the doors at either end of the shed wide open. As I was unloading, I heard the Happymount Express coming around; I looked back and saw it approaching on the curve with about a half-load of passengers.

I waved as it passed. If Len saw me, he didn't acknowledge it.

Now, I'm not pretending that I'd suddenly seen the light back there when we'd talked in the shed. But I had gone in with a pretty one-dimensional attitude to his character based entirely on Big Brian's account, and seeing that inept little tableau had forced me to rethink. All right, so it was crap. But he'd taken the trouble to set it up. The man had a creative urge, even if he had no talent; and the point was that I could no longer despise him in quite the way that I had when I'd known nothing about him.

And I suppose there was a vanity angle to it as well. Here was this obstacle course in human relations, as Big Brian had described him, and yet my simple little suggestion had broken through. I was like the teacher of the Wild Boy of Aveyron, except that my success had been with the Fat Sod of Happymount. Thorns and lions' paws would be as nothing to me after this. As I was stacking everything by Len's workbench inside, the train came through again and I stepped back into darkness until it had passed by.

I had to walk past the figure of the miner to get out, and it was only when I reached the open air that I could identify the unease I'd been feeling.

I'd assumed that it was something territorial, a sense of being less than welcome in someone else's place.

But it wasn't.

Crap or not, and no matter how unlifelike, it was more as if the figure had been waiting for me to leave.

* * *

'Get a gallon can of that grey undercoat and meet me up behind the Mister Men,' Big Brian ordered me one day, and there was something in his voice that made me get up off my seat in the brew hut without a smart remark.

The Mister Men were a series of figures up at the highest point in the park, set around a crescent that itself was built around an ornamental flower bed. The figures all had names, but I couldn't tell you what any of them were. They were basically just different-coloured blobs with faces. Behind them were bushes, and behind the bushes was the perimeter fence. Big Brian was waiting there for me, his face filled with troubled fury at the latest doings of the Yob Element.

'Look at this,' he said to me. 'Is this a sign of a tiny mind, or what?'

I looked.

The tiny mind in question had set itself to the task of writing the words *Toe Cap Ted* along with a few more notions of even deeper mystery on the back of one of the flats. I think it was magic marker. Down at the bottom of the flat there was evidence of a half-hearted attempt to set it alight, but the flame-retardant paint had barely charred. Spent matches were scattered all around, along with a few empty Woodpecker Cider cans that had been crushed and bent double. It didn't look like it had been much of a party.

Big Brian said, 'They write their own names as if they're something special, but they have to hide before they can feel big enough to do it. They make me sick. Get it all painted out.'

'Is it worth it? They can always come back.'

'I'll be watching for them if they do,' he said darkly, and clambered out through the scaffolding as I set down my can of undercoat and levered off the top.

The job didn't take more than ten minutes but I didn't enjoy doing it, any more than I enjoyed picking up the litter. It was too much like being a lackey for whoever had made the mess, with me being stuck here while they moved on to other, equally trivial pleasures. I could take a guess at who'd done it, although it was only a guess; there were three only-just teenagers who came into the park every now and again, plug-ugly and with the dress sense of a circus geek, laughing and shoving each other and swearing out loud to shock anyone who might be listening. There was nothing here for them, so they never stayed long; the park was basically just somewhere to go. Even if they weren't the ones responsible, they were close enough to type for it not to matter. Kids with nothing to say, saying it loud.

The reason that I'm making so much of this is that I saw the three of them again the next evening, and they were down by the railway. I'd been walking by and wondering what kind of progress Len had been making, thinking that maybe I could wait until he was collecting the ticket money over on the far side of the track and then take a quick peek inside the shed without his knowledge, when I spotted them on the path that ran alongside the track for a way. One shoved another, the other bawled *Fuck off, spunkface* and attempted one of those aimless kung-fu kicks that was always a sure sign of having sneaked into too many Bruce Lee movies, the first one dodged, the third one laughed like an emptying drain.

And then around came Len, the big man on the little engine with his toddlers all riding behind. If you've ever seen one of those circus cycling acts where they bring out a tiny tricycle about the size of a roller skate and one of the acrobats hunkers down with his knees up alongside his ears and pedals it along for a few yards. . . well, that was almost how he looked as the Happymount Express came around the bend.

I was more than a hundred yards away but I stopped and watched, fascinated, almost like an astronomer watching a couple of stars on their way toward an imminent collision. The boys heard the train coming and glanced back; I couldn't see Len's face but I could imagine that it would be set like stone, staring dead ahead.

They all started making train noises. One of them tried to sing *Casey Junior's comin' down the track*, which I think was in Dumbo, but he messed up the words.

And another one jumped in front of the train, waving his arms.

I'm sure that if it had been at all possible to put on a burst of acceleration, Len would have done it and run the boy down. As it was, the Express chugged along at its regular speed and the boy jumped off the track after a fraction of a second, walking away with about twenty-five yards to spare. As a feat of daring, it basically wasn't; and then the three of them had all turned their backs and were drifting off in a careful piece of timing that said look at me, I'm not running, while dodging the prospect of a direct confrontation.

The Express slowed, and then it stopped.

I'd never before seen Len stop the train anywhere other than in the shed or at the station platform. The boys heard it, but they didn't turn; even so, I saw them tense with apprehension as events began to move in a direction they hadn't expected.

Len stood up on the engine. Behind him one or two of the smallest children tried to get out thinking that the ride was over, only to be restrained by their parents.

'Boys!' Len called. 'Oh, *boys!* Yes, I'm talking to you!'

I wouldn't have called it a friendly tone. That's how it sounded on the surface but underneath, it was anything but.

They could hardly pretend not to have heard, and there was no-one else in the immediate area. They turned, cowed and caught-out looking.

'I'm just about to close down for the night,' Len said, and if I hadn't known better I'd have said that he sounded downright genial. 'One more run, and then that's it. Now, I see you're quite interested in the railway. So how about one last ride? On the house?'

They all hesitated. Their faces were drained and slack. If I can say it without being too unkind, these boys were not Nobel Prize contenders and were unlikely ever to become such; Len's irony was wasted on them.

And so they puffed themselves up in an attempt to recover some trace of their stolen bravado, swallowed the bait and, rather selfconsciously, climbed into the last empty carriages at the end of the train.

I watched as the Happymount Express chugged past me and away. The three of them were sitting with their knees up in the tiny carriages and trying to look cool and at their ease, already laughing again; Hey, a free ride from the fat man, are we the bee's nuts or what? But they couldn't see that, even as they'd climbed aboard, they'd been conceding victory to Len without even being aware of it.

I didn't see the train as it reached the platform. But when it reappeared, moving along track through the most distant part of the woodland, I could see that everyone else had disembarked save Len and, right at the end of the carriages, the three boys.

I watched them as the Express chugged through the trees and then on into the tunnel.

And then I waited, but it didn't come out.

So I waited a while longer.

And still nothing came out.

Oh, shit.

By now I was seriously beginning to wonder whether I ought to go and tell Big Brian. I couldn't imagine what might be going on in there. . or rather, I could, and it owed rather more to Hammer Films and the Chamber of Horrors than to any likely version of reality. There were no screams, no noises, nothing. All that I could hear were the faint strains of taped music from the kiddies' carousel, all the way back across the park alongside the cafeteria. Perhaps, I started to think nervously, I ought to go over there and take a look. And if I found the shed doors closed then I'd. . . I'd. . .

Well, afterwards I could imagine all of the heroic and responsible things that I surely would have done, because at that moment I saw the first of the boys emerging from the far end of the shed. I couldn't see his face, but his entire attitude was that of a beaten dog in a state of shock. The others skulked after. One of them looked back, and I've never seen anyone quite so pale. They all looked as if they were walking on hot sand, in shoes that were too thin.

I couldn't help it. I had to go over to the engine shed.

By the time that I got there, Len was almost ready to leave. I stood by the tracks just inside the open doorway, hesitating to walk any further uninvited; he was over at the table, packing his empty lunchbox and the rest of his stuff into his duffel bag, but he looked up and saw me. For a second his face was dull and ugly, but then he smiled. It wasn't much of an improvement.

And it wasn't a pleased-to-see-you smile, either. I said, 'What happened?'

If he was pleased with anybody, it was with himself. 'I only did what their parents should have done a long time ago,' he said, picking up the duffel bag and moving over to the engine. There he unscrewed the brass operating handle and put it into the bag to take home with him, effectively immobilising the train. Maybe you could have done something with a spanner to get around it, I really don't know, but for all practical purposes it was like taking the clutch pedal out of a car. 'I explained a few things to them and rubbed their snotty little noses in the facts of life. Showed them what they'd get if they crossed me again. They won't be back in a hurry.'

As he walked past me and out into the daylight, I could smell diesel oil and corruption. I hadn't gone any way towards liking the man, not at all, but I had begun to think that perhaps he couldn't be as bad as Big Brian had described him. But not any more. I'd no reason to feel anything for those three boys; but somehow, I was desperately glad that I hadn't had to share any of the last few minutes with them.

I glanced around before I followed Len out. I was wondering what exactly he might have said to them; somehow the old bones-and-oildrum routine didn't seem enough to explain their reaction. I could see where he'd been working on the goldmine tableau, although he hadn't made much in the way of progress at all. The figure had changed position slightly and had been daubed with even more fluorescent paint, and Len had added some chickenwire and newspaper boulders and a couple of crates with *Dinermite* stencilled onto the sides. He'd painted skulls on the walls. He'd dug out a shallow trench to hide the UV tube - or the dandruff light, as they called them in the local discos, because they showed up every fleck and fibre and made your teeth glow like Liberace's - and he'd made a start at burying the tannoy wiring, which I almost tripped over because he'd threaded it under the tracks and hung the loudspeaker alongside the door. The wiring ran all the way back to the workshop area, but didn't seem to have been connected to anything yet.

Above the workbench hung three dead rats, dangling by their tails in a bunch.

Suddenly I wanted to be out of it, now. It was like a small child's nightmare of the Batcave in there. The crudity of it all made it worse. They say that artists reveal themselves through their work, whether they mean to or not; and if this was a peek into Len's head, then I preferred not to dwell on the details. It was like seeing a fish cut open, and its insides found to be teeming with parasitic worms.

He was waiting as I emerged. As soon as I was out, he closed and padlocked the big doors after me.

And I said I had to be somewhere, so that I wouldn't have to stay in his company as the two of us walked away.

* * *

Here's what happened then.

It was a Monday, about two weeks later. The preceding weekend had been the last to feature the illuminations, and the final switchoff had taken place on the previous night. Big Brian had gone around and taken out all of the fuses, and wouldn't be putting them back. This was the day that we were due to start taking everything apart to go back into storage until next year.

I knew as soon as I got in that something was wrong, because there was a police car alongside the Mad Hatter's Tea Party and a uniformed man inside talking to Big Brian. I hung back, not wanting to walk in and interrupt but wondering if there might be some way that I could just, kind of, *sidle in* at the back and pick up on what was going on without actually getting involved, when another police van went past behind me at rather more than the park regulation speed of ten miles per hour. It carried on down the boulevard, and I followed it.

There was quite a crowd building up. Well, when I say quite a crowd, I mean quite a crowd for Happymount Park on a dull Monday morning; two or three dozen people, at least, and they were all craning for a better look at whatever was going on around Len's engine shed. More police vehicles had been driven off the pathways and into the woodland, and they'd been parked - probably deliberately - in a way that screened the main doors from view. And just in case anyone got any ideas about getting closer, there was a man in uniform standing with his arms folded and his beady eyes daring them to try it. Behind him, two more men were staking out the area with plastic tape.

I spotted somebody I knew.

His name was Simon and he'd been at school around the same time as me, although in a different class. When he'd left he'd been taken on by the local newspaper as tea-maker and general office-boy, and after a while he'd progressed to coverage of all the wedding anniversaries. But that hardly seemed to be his purpose here.

He came up alongside me and said, 'What's your angle on all of this, then?'

And I said, 'I haven't got an angle. What's supposed to have happened?'

But instead of telling me, he lost interest and wandered off. I don't think he actually knew, at least not yet. I think they'd sent him out to the scene without any guidance on how to tackle the job. From Silver Weddings to suspicious death, in one uneasy leap. I actually found out the details from Big Brian later on, when the police had finished and a big lorry had come to take away the engine of the Happymount Express to be stripped down and checked.

Len Cunningham had been discovered by one of the gardeners that morning, face-down on the track about ten yards outside the engine shed. The train was half-out of its tunnel like a snake emerging from a hole in the ground. The way they reconstructed it, he'd been crouched on the track inside doing something with the tannoy wire when the train had somehow rolled forward and caught him. He must have had his head right down, and hadn't seen or heard it coming at all; it was almost like being sucked into a blender. It pushed him out of the shed while dragging him under at the same time, so that his head and arm had finished up about halfway along under the engine. They weren't clean off, but apparently nobody had dared to pull too hard when they'd been lifting him off the track. And he hadn't died straight away, either, if the signs of clawing all the way alongside the trackbed were anything to go by.

All of this had happened late the previous evening, probably when the park lights had been out and the rest of us were going home. They reckoned that he might not even have been able to make a sound. He'd been lying there all night, and his torn coat was heavy with dew. Someone who'd seen him told me what he'd looked like, and I don't care to think about it too much. The police were interested because, without a driver's hand on the Dead Man's Handle, the train shouldn't have been able to move.

But somehow, it would seem, it had done exactly that.

I'll tell you my first reaction, and that was to think about the three boys who'd been given that one last ride of their childhood; but they'd all been somewhere else for the biggest part of the evening, and there were witnesses who could prove it. They were at a pantomime, no less. The one with a goose in it.

Taking it all together, it was one of the park's more interesting days. The rest of us tried to work around the activity, but inevitably very little got done. I spent most of the day just trying to believe what I'd heard. Even though I saw Old Jack being let in to spread sand on the trackbed where it had happened, I still had trouble making the story connect with reality.

Late on in the day, I saw Old Jack talking to one of the policemen. When they'd finished, Old Jack came over to me and said, 'They're all done here. You can lock the shed up, now.'

Me? Old Jack went mooching off, and I went looking for Big Brian. He was up on a scaffolding, taking down the skyline of Toytown with the help of a couple of council electricians who'd come along to put it all up at the beginning of the season.

'The police are all finished,' I called up to him. 'They want us to lock up the shed.'

He looked down at me, and I could see that the two hundred pounds of painted board that he was supporting made this an inconvenient moment. I could already guess what he was going to say.

'See to it, will you?'

'It ought to be someone in charge,' I offered lamely.

'Did anyone say that?'

But nobody had.

Dead Man's Handle

'Go on, then,' he said. 'Nothing's going to bite you.'

And so I went to get the key.

The tapes were down, but a couple of scraps of it were still blowing about. The park gates had been closed, and no-one was hanging around now. The engine shed hadn't exactly been Sleeping Beauty's palace before, but now it had all the appeal of an abattoir. Both ends were open. I was going to have to bolt one set of doors from the inside, and then walk the length of it in the dark. When I went to switch on the few available lights, I saw the scattered sand and I saw the marks where Len Cunningham had scrabbled at the trackbed in the last few seconds of his life. So its end hadn't been quick, and it hadn't been painless, and here was the proof.

The bolts squealed like gallows chains. That's the kind of mood the place had put me in.

As I was walking back up the track, I could see along the engineless carriages to the tableau at the far end. I wasn't looking forward to having to pass it. Len appeared to have rearranged everything a little more, moving the figure again and changing the lights, and I wished that he hadn't; as before the figure was unnatural and astonishingly ugly, and the effect now was as if it had moved when I hadn't been looking. The only way that I can describe my feelings as I approached it would be to go back to a number of years before and the first time that I'd ever been into a waxworks, a really cheesy one in New Brighton where the figures all looked like painted deathmasks and none of them taken from the people that they were supposed to represent. The building itself had been run-down and damp, its timbers so rotten that all of the floors creaked when you walked over them. . . and with certain boards, in certain places, you could walk over a spot on the floor and, in some totally different part of the room, one or other of the figures would slowly begin to lean forward.

Well, this one didn't really move. At least, not while I was looking. But it gave me exactly that same, slow-burning scare as I approached it, and as soon as I got to the end of the carriages I crossed over the tracks so that I'd pass by it on the other side.

I must have tripped a switch down on the trackbed, intended to be kicked over by the train itself. The tannoy speaker crackled into life and I looked around wildly for a moment before I realised what was happening; the sound of a pick rang out on stone, a shovel plunged into gravel, and I realised that I'd triggered Len's over-amplified cassette tape of atmospheric mine effects. A faint voice cried out, *Look out, it's all gonna fall*, and there was an avalanche effect that sounded like a few rocks being emptied out of a zinc bucket. The voice was unmistakably Len Cunningham's.

It was all so utterly fucking spooky.

And now the lurching, falling-forward figure of the gold miner was grinning at me.

It took a moment to register exactly what I was seeing. The shapeless hat and the bristles that had concealed his features were gone. He was grinning because he had no choice; because his face was a day-glo painted skull and his eyes were two pitted golfballs, probably boosted from the Crazy Golf hut at the far end of the gardens. Dark pupils had been drawn onto them like cartoon eyes. Two teeth were missing. And in the gaps between his coatsleeves and his heavy workman's gloves, I could see not the broomhandles that I'd have expected but a slender inch of bone.

Look out, it's all gonna fall, the dead man cried as the tape loop went around again.

It stood there, almost daring me to come closer.

I was looking at what I would later learn were the remains of a teenager named Keith Mills, slightly retarded, missing presumed dead. Tests on the bones showed that they'd been boiled for several hours. Of all the people who'd been in and out of the engine shed in the course of the day, not one of them could have given the figure more than a passing glance.

I was out of there faster than a cat out of a bonfire.

I don't know how long it took before Big Brian was able to get any sense out of me. But when the police came back again and wanted me to walk over to the shed with them, I'm told that they couldn't get me to go. I was in a state. To be perfectly honest, I don't remember very much of the next couple of hours until my father arrived to take me home. And every time I tried to talk to anyone about it, I stopped making sense. This lasted for more than a week.

And, as I said, I've been getting bad dreams about it ever since.

The police gave me a hard time. They were sure I'd been messing around. I think a lot of it was to cover their own embarrassment at the way they'd trudged through their procedures and yet missed something so obvious. They said that I'd tampered with the figure. Which, of course, I hadn't.

But I can see why they'd think that I had.

I'd only stared at it for a matter of seconds, but the picture's still vivid in my mind after all these years. That unreal glow of blue and orange in the UV light. That grin. Those golfball eyes. How that shapeless old hat was now missing from the figure's head; and how in its place there now sat an engine driver's cap.

The big shadows on the wall behind it. The sense of triumph in its attitude.

The presence of Death.

With a well-worn brass handle in its hand.

GUILTY PARTY

by

Stephen Laws

'I've been a wild rover for many a year,
And I've spent all me money on whiskey and beer,
But now I've returned with gold in great store,
I won't play the wild rover. No never.
No more.'

The last chorus of the old song reverberated from the battered mini-bus as it sped swaying down yet another country lane. As if on cue, a sudden turn in the road sent the chorus leader, who had been standing in the aisle, crashing across two of the seats.

There was a roar of drunken laughter.

It had been a good night. The usual office Christmas party with hired bus and a pub far out in the wilds. Stamfordham was usually a quiet little spot. Not really too remote, but 'countryfied' enough to appeal to the most hardened of 'city' types and to arouse the irritation of local residents when the Newcastle 'townies' arrived en masse to take over the only two pubs in the area.

Stuart heaved himself from the seat and struggled past Mark towards the back of the bus. Mark by this time had begun to lead the others in another typical 'Oirish' folk song: 'The Wild Colonial Boy' - and the strains of the boozy singers echoed in Stuart's whisky befuddled brain as he slumped next to Steve, who was near to falling asleep, partly because of the rocking of the bus but mainly because of the ten rum and cokes which had passed through his system.

Moonlight occasionally flashed through the ragged trees which reared and loomed past the windows as the bus rattled on its way, city-bound.

'Hello, my good man,' said Steve slurrily. 'What brings you down here then?'

'Just had an idea,' said Stuart. 'An idea for a story.'

Both men were fanatical dreamers and film buffs. Ideas for scripts and screenplays were often shouted across the office in between writing reports and drafting committee minutes.

'Just supposing,' Stuart went on after a slight pause, 'that there's been an office party just like this one, and we're on our way home. Just like this. Then, suddenly, one of the people on the bus sees something... *something*... outside in the trees, by the glare of the headlights.'

Steve pursed his lips thoughtfully and screwed up his eyebrows. Then, after another pause he looked at Stuart.

'You mean... something vague. Something... not quite *right*.'

'Yeah. That's right. Something pretty weird. So that he's not sure whether it's the booze or not.'

'It would be a good starting point for...'

'... a horror film. Yeah.'

They continued to bounce ideas off each other. Clichés abounded. Stock situations seemed to spring readily to mind. Completely absorbed, they'd forgotten everything else. Suddenly, a chorus of voices brought Stuart back to reality.

'Stuart! Hi, man! You don't want to sleep on the bus tonight, do you? It's your stop!'

'Is it?'

Stuart bundled to his feet and pulled his coat on.

'Don't forget, Steve! This is one we can take up on Monday. See you!'

As he bustled to the front of the bus, a flurry of arms slapped him amiably across the shoulders.

'Get a move on, Stu! We've got to get home as well, you know!'

The hiss of the pneumatic bus door. The bite of the cold winter air. With breath turning to steam, Stuart turned on the step and waved his arm in a mock dramatic gesture of farewell.

As he stepped down from the bus and into the night, the cries of farewell were snuffed out as the door snapped shut. With a coughing roar of the engine, a shifting of gears and a crunch of gravel, the bus sped off rattling into the blackness of the country lane.

Country lane?

What the hell am I doing in a country lane? thought Stuart, spinning none too steadily on one heel and surveying the blue blackness of his surroundings. In the cold moonlight he could just make out a row of hedges bristling on each side of the road.

Clutches of trees like gnarled giants crouched along the roadway, their spiny fingers dancing in the freezing air as if conducting the weird melody which the wind was playing amongst them.

Guilty Party

'The stupid idiots have dropped me off in a country-bloody road! Miles from anywhere.'

It was a little while before he realised that he was standing directly under a rusted signpost and when he squinted up at the weather-beaten lettering, he realised what had happened.

'Don't forget,' he had said in the Bay Horse Pub, 'I've got to be dropped off at Crawpost when we head back. My mate's picking me up there and taking me on home.'

The signpost had only two place-names on it... Newcastle 13 miles: Crowfast Farm 2 miles. Maybe Crawpost *had* sounded like Crowfast after ten whiskies but it didn't make Stuart feel any better disposed towards his fellow man as he started to walk down the lane. Turning up his collar he looked for a telephone box or the tell-tale flashing headlights of an approaching car. Nothing. Not even the distant glow from a farmhouse window.

Nothing.

He began to curse under his breath that the party had been organised so far away from Newcastle. Why couldn't it have been held in the town? Or at least near to a bus route. Here he was, miles from anywhere on a lonely country road. Anything could happen. He could fall into a ditch and break a leg or something. Unnoticed for weeks maybe. That was a good idea for a story...

Stories later. The first matter of priority was a phone box or a farmhouse with a telephone.

Only ten minutes had passed, when a gradual feeling of unease began to creep over him. Continually, he found himself glancing over at the other side of the road as the hedges hissed and swayed in the wind. Stuart was not a nervous man. Admittedly, being stranded out in the wilds was an irritating experience to say the least, but no reason to suppose that someone was...

Damn it, someone *was* following him! Creeping along behind the hedge on the other side of the road.

Stuart stopped. This was bloody stupid. There wasn't anyone there. *This is what comes of getting ideas for horror films,* he thought. He continued to walk, the lonely sound of his footsteps on the road somehow challenging the darkness. But he still couldn't lose the feeling that something was moving over there.

Must be a cow.

Another five minutes or so passed as he walked. For an instant, he thought he saw something slinking past a gap in the hedgerow. Again, he stopped and stared at the hedge. there wasn't anybody there, surely? Funny thing though, standing there in the moonlight staring at the hedgerow as he was, Stuart had to admit that by a trick of the light it *did* look as if something was just visible on the other side. Something that crouched and watched.

Stuart laughed and kept on walking. He conjured up pictures of Cary Grant in a similar situation. Alighting from a bus in the film 'North by Northwest', he had found himself out in the open. Isolated and vulnerable. And then he'd been attacked by a crop-dusting aeroplane.

But that was in the daytime. No homicidal plane pilot in sight here. Just a rustling in the hedgerow which seemed to be keeping pace with him as he walked.

Unconsciously, he found himself walking slightly into the road; away from the gravel at the roadside which had been crunching underfoot. Was he afraid of giving away his position? Could that be his own shadow somehow reflecting in the shrubbery? No... his own shadow was right there in the middle of the road. The foolishness of the situation stopped him from crossing the lane and peering over the hedge.

A scudding cloud covered the moon like a giant veil and the countryside was plunged into an even greater darkness.

Stuart had read the clichés about fear jolting a person's nervous system like an electric shock. He had heard how a person's blood could 'turn to ice' and of how his heart could 'leap into his mouth.' But he was totally unprepared for it to happen to him.

As if waiting for the moon to disappear, something large crashed through the hedge and was bounding across the road. What happened next seemed to be a series of impressions... of 'frozen frames' in a film. Everything happened so quickly. Something came dashing at him through the dark. Something which panted heavy and loud as it approached. Stuart was frozen in his tracks. In an instant, he had the horrific impression that something *wanted* to catch him very desperately. Something altogether bestial, hungry and decidedly unpleasant. A glint in the dark from what seemed to be an eye or a tooth made him realise that his assailant was almost on top of him. Almost at his ear there came an animal-like snarl and a brush of hair on his cheek as he ducked down instinctively onto his haunches. He was not a moment too soon. The slashing blow aimed at his face missed - and ripped the cloth on the back of his jacket. And then there was a crush of undergrowth as his night enshrouded attacker burst through the other hedge behind him.

Stuart wheeled around to face the hedge just as the moon reappeared, throwing out everything around him in stark black and white. A gaping hole had been torn in the hedge, the inner fringes of which still twisted and writhed from the passage of... whatever it had been.

Stuart could actually feel his heart pounding in his chest. His throat seemed dry and constricted. He was no longer drunk.

An impression remained in his mind of a man-like shape. But not a man.

'No...' Stuart muttered under his breath, his eyes flickering the length of the hedgerow, '... not a werewolf either. More like some stupid bugger dressed in a ridiculous werewolf costume from a very bad horror B-feature.'

It all seemed perfectly clear. Somebody was dressed up and trying to scare the hell out of him. Well... he'd done a pretty good job so far. If Stuart hadn't left Steve on the bus, he would have sworn that this would be the sort of trick *he* would pull after their conversation on film plots.

Stuart started to run, still scanning the bushes at his left, not sure whether the sound of his own gasping covered the horrific panting and growling of something keeping abreast with him on the other side of the hedge. Hardly even altering his speed, he stooped and grabbed half of a housebrick from the grass verge. Still running, he weighed the brick in his hand. The very fact that it was a housebrick and not just some rock was a comfort. A brick made by a builder for a house. For people. Out in the wilds, it was a comfort to know that his grab for a weapon had given him something which was man-made. Now, even the lonely stretch of road didn't seem quite so cut off from civilisation as before, and the feeling that there was nothing more supernatural than a lunatic in a halloween costume following him, made Stuart's fear re-channel itself into something approaching rage. Just one more glimpse of the bastard, and he'd have a skull fracture to laugh off.

Stuart's anger reached a peak. Veering in towards a gap in the hedge where anyone on the other side would have to pass, he suddenly halted, whirled and raised the brick ready to throw.

Just show yourself for one second...

Sucking in lungfuls of air, he tensed... waiting for his assailant. His own heartbeats thudded like the footsteps of an approaching giant.

Nothing.

Clouds of breath streamed around his face.

Nothing.

The branches of a nearby tree shook and rattled in the wind.

Nothing.

Slowly, Stuart began to move along the road again, still with the brick half raised in his hand, ever watchful for any sign of movement. A flicker of light between the trees suddenly caught his eye.

A farm! Crowfast Farm!

He realised that he'd run almost two miles. Normally, running for a bus would have completely winded him. But the circumstances here were entirely different. If the farm had a telephone - which it surely must have - he could 'phone for a taxi and be on his way home in no time at all. On instinct, Stuart turned quickly as he ran. About twenty-five yards behind him something suddenly dashed across the road from right to left and vanished into a copse of trees. Something which crouched as it ran, but with extremely broad shoulders and long arms. And... pointed ears?

Stuart began to run even faster than before. The road twisted to the right and, just at the turn, he saw on the left-hand side a twisted, roughly hewn gate bearing a hand-etched inscription... 'Crowfast Farm'.

Deep in the trees he could see the glow which had first caught his eye. Reaching the gate, Stuart took a running leap by bracing one hand on the topmost bar of the gate. Years of sitting behind a desk and insufficient exercise suddenly caught up with him as his foot caught against the bar and sent him cartwheeling into the deep grass on the other side of the gate. Spitting out soil, he pulled himself to his feet. His left leg felt about six inches longer than the other one. The thought of being hemmed in by trees was suddenly unnerving. At least in the open road he could almost see if anyone was lurking nearby. But with all of those trees...

Crashing into the copse, Stuart dodged in and out around the tree trunks with his eyes fixed steadfastly on the glowing light up ahead. No less than ten yards into the trees he heard something blundering into the gate behind him.

Bastard!

Guilty Party

Spinning around, Stuart swung his arm back to throw the brick and for the first time really saw his pursuer, crouched at the gate and with the moonlight shining full on its face.

As a child, Stuart had once dreamed that someone was standing in the shadows at the foot of his bed. Frozen by some strange force, he had watched as the figure silently moved around the bed and approached him. It was only when the figure had suddenly thrust itself forward into the moonlight that he had been able to scream and pull the bedclothes over his head. The same immobility now came over him as he saw - the slavering jaws, the balefully glowing red eyes, and the hideously pointed wolf's ears.

This was no lunatic in a halloween costume...

The stooping figure paused at the broken gate and swung its head backwards and forwards, looking for him. The clawed arms swung restlessly like some horrific ape. The figure suddenly became rigid and Stuart realised that it had seen him. As the horror, with terrible strength, loped over the gate and lunged into the trees towards him, the spell broke and Stuart heaved the brick with more strength than he thought he had. At once, he knew that he had thrown wide of the mark. He watched as the projectile twisted through the air, as if in slow motion. The man-beast thrashed between the trees and it seemed as if the missile would hit one of the tree boles. Unaware of the projectile, the beast stepped straight into its path.

The brick struck the animal full on the temple with an audible crunch of bone and sent it reeling into the undergrowth. Turning, Stuart dashed through the trees and was suddenly aware of the most chilling howl of rage and pain from behind him. He had never heard a wolf howl before. Only on film. Never in real life. Again, the thought came back to him that he had been caught in the fantasy world of a B-film character.

But for no more than an instant. This nightmare was real. The iced air tore at his lungs as he charged through the undergrowth. The tangled grass and weeds seemed to deliberately clutch at his legs, slowing him down.

The farmhouse *must* be up ahead somewhere. The light flashed clearly through the trees only twenty yards away. From somewhere behind him came the sound of crashing vegetation. only ten yards to go. A thicket obscured the light. Clawing fingers. Twigs tearing at his clothes. Thrusting through the shrubbery, Stuart came into a small clearing and saw the source of the light.

'What the bloody hell...?'

A lantern hung from the low limb of an ash tree, throwing out the surrounding trees in bright relief. A lantern, but no farm house.

Jesus! There had to be a farmhouse somewhere. Realising that he'd run into the copse only to find that there was no sanctuary and that the thing behind him was still approaching rapidly made panic clutch at his throat. There *must* be a farmhouse nearby. Who had put the light there? And why? Stuart dashed around the clearing frantically searching for some sign of human habitation.

The farmhouse was up ahead, surrounded on all sides by thick undergrowth and twisted trees. Stuart had a fleeting glimpse of dilapidated buildings, a crumbling wall and rusting farm equipment as he launched himself towards the main thatched building. A dull light shone through one of its windows. The solid oak door seemed to swing towards him at a crazy angle as he pounded into a small paved yard, leapt over the rusting plough and crashed against the panelling. Grasping the large gargoyle door-knocker, he pounded on the door.

'Let me in!'

Looking over his shoulder as he hammered on the solid oak, he saw a dark shadow lurching through the trees just beyond the glow of the lantern in the clearing.

'*Let me in!*'

As he pounded, he realised that the creature could easily find him by the noise he was making. They were the longest moments Stuart had ever experienced in his life. A crash from somewhere behind, and the yellow glow of the lantern was extinguished.

'*LET ME IN!*'

Suddenly, there came the judder and rattle of a large bolt being thrown on the other side of the door, and Stuart practically fell inside as the heavy door swung inwards. A hand grasped his arm to steady him as he staggered across a musty room and into a chair. The door slammed shut and he heard the bolt being pushed back into position. Gasping for breath, Stuart looked up and saw a small and very wrinkled old man with an extremely benign face and faded-blue eyes standing at the door holding a small lantern above his stooped head. Its guttering light made shadows loom and sway throughout the room.

The old man smiled.

'Happy Birthday, son. We've been expecting you.'

Stuart pointed at the window, unable to speak, as he sucked in lungfuls of the stale air. The old man slowly followed his pointing finger, smiling again, and crossed to the far side of the room to a battered door. In the gloom, Stuart could just make out the ancient furniture in the room. A gigantic cobweb stretched from an old spinning wheel in the corner to a dust covered sideboard.

The old man opened the door and without taking his eyes from his visitor, called to someone beyond.

'Violet. He's come.'

Stuart stood up, chest heaving, and moved to the fly-stained window. The faint light from the within the room cast a faint reflection out into the yard but the blackness beyond hid anything that might... that *was* lurking outside.

'Listen,' Stuart said and turned again to the old man, who had shut the door and moved to the table in the centre of the room, 'Have you got a 'phone?'

The old man smiled.

'A phone? Have you got a phone?' Stuart demanded angrily. 'There's a dangerous animal out there. Somebody's got to 'phone the police!'

'You know we haven't got a 'phone, Matthew,' said the old man.

The door behind him opened with a slight creak and an old woman appeared, stooped and shambling. Stuart could see that her face held the same indulgent smile as that of the old man. Her eyes lit up as she looked at Stuart from under a furrowed brow.

'Matthew,' she said, 'we knew that you'd come back to us. Happy Birthday, son.'

Stuart braced himself and looked at the couple, anger beginning to swell inside.

'I'm not Matthew, whoever he is. And if we don't do something...'

Another figure entered the room. A younger man with a checked shirt and a notably extravagant expression of grim determination. However, the most notable thing about him was the 12 bore shotgun which he held - pointed at Stuart's chest.

The old man placed a hand on Stuart's shoulder.

'Sit down, my boy.'

As he sat, the younger man shut the door with his foot and hissed at the old woman: 'Is it him?'

The old lady smiled, nodded and pulled up a chair at the table across from Stuart and the old man.

This is crazy! thought Stuart.

'Ten years to the day, Matthew,' croaked the old man, 'and here you are, just as you said you would be. You always were true to your word. Punctuality. Punct-u-ality.'

Stuart began to stand again. The younger man waved the shotgun in a gesture which made Stuart realise that not only was there great danger outside, but also a very real danger *inside*.

'Would you mind telling me just what's going on?' he asked

'You *know*, Matthew. It's been a long time now since we last saw you. And I suppose we should really explain a few things. You have every right to be angry with us for what we did, but it was all for the best. All for the best.' Stuart sat down again and the old man crossed his arms on the table, before continuing. 'If you hadn't been such a wild rover in the first place, Matthew, nothing would have come of it. But... when you returned to your mother and I after all those years abroad we *were* glad to see you again.' The old man pointed at the younger man with the gun. 'Arnold always missed his brother, didn't you Arnold? And as for all that money you brought back with you... It's still here, you know. We've never touched a bit of it. Locked up in the cellar for ten years, it's been. "Matthew's money" --- that's what your mother calls it. We've been keeping it for you.'

Stuart shifted uncomfortably in his seat and glanced at the window.

The old man continued: 'So we've never stolen anything, son. You've got to understand that we didn't kill you for your money.'

Stuart looked at the old man again. He *must* be mad.

'We really didn't want to kill you in the first place. But you know how it was when you came back to us. You were changed. And when the killings started - well, we did shelter you. Didn't we? We would never have given you away, would we, mother? We suffered for a long time, Matthew. The old gypsy lady told us what was happening and what we should do. When the little boy was killed, we had no alternative...'

The old lady leaned forward. 'We were never cruel parents, Matthew. Were we father?'

'No, of course we weren't.' The old man shook his head slowly and earnestly. 'But anyway... you're here now, just like you said you would be. And you're not angry with us anymore for what we did.'

Stuart turned to the younger man. 'Listen, mate. There's an animal out there. It looks like a... well, it's... You've got to get a message to the police or something. Have you got a car?'

The young man remained impassive, shotgun still pointed at him.

'We can't have a birthday without a birthday party, can we, Violet?' said the old man.

Smiling like a small child who has just thought of a new game to play, the old woman scurried past the shotgun-wielding Arnold and into the darkness beyond.

'I'm not your son,' protested Stuart. 'You should know that. My name's...'

'Of course you are, Matthew,' replied the old man indulgently.

'Look, I don't even... Have you got a picture? A picture of your son?'

Arnold stood slightly to one side and motioned with the shotgun at a picture hanging over the spinning wheel.

'I can't see it clearly.'

Stretching across, Arnold took down the picture and gingerly placed it in front of Stuart, the barrels of the shotgun coming uncomfortably close to his face. Wiping the dust from the glass frame, Stuart saw that the face was of a very ordinary looking young man in his mid-twenties. Glassy eyes. Dark hair. The likeness to the threatening young man with the gun was unmistakable.

'Brother?' Stuart asked.

For the first time, Arnold spoke. In a voice that quivered with fear.

'Yes.'

'Listen, old man,' said Stuart, 'this picture doesn't even remotely look like me.'

The old man wagged a reproachful finger at Stuart. 'The gypsy lady said that you would be changed when you came back. Being able to change was always one of your tricks, you know.'

The woman returned from her mission carrying a wooden tray. On the tray rested a cake. A huge birthday cake covered in candles, many of which were cracked and broken. A wickedly sharp cake knife lay alongside it. Stuart could see that the cake itself was old. Very old. Cobwebs fluttered on its surface. Through the mould, he could just make out that the cake had once been decorated with the legend, 'Happy Birthday Matthew'.

The old man gestured to Arnold to sit down with them at the table. As he sat, the woman handed him a party hat and then, reaching across the table, gave another to Stuart and the old man. The old man smoothed it onto his balding pate. A green hat with long spikes that rustled in the still air like a strange crown.

'Come on, Matthew. Join in the fun.'

Stuart again rose to his feet, pushing the chair back as he did so.

'If you think...'

Arnold leapt to his feet and swung the shotgun up.

'Sit down, Matthew.'

The old man gripped Stuart by the coatsleeve.

'Sit... *down* and join in the fun,' he hissed vehemently through clenched teeth, the air of gentility completely gone from his voice. Stuart sat, slowly and reluctantly, putting the orange paper hat on his head. The old lady had begun to light the candles on the cake.

'It has to be done this way,' hissed the old man. 'The old lady said so. When you promised to come back to us, Matt... as you were dying... you were very angry. You would have killed us. The old lady said that you would come back on your birthday. Today. And that if we didn't arrange things properly, there wouldn't be... wouldn't be any stopping you. You do see that don't you son?' The tone of the old man's voice had changed again. Now he was imploring Stuart, trying to make him understand. 'You've got to have a special cake ready for him when he returns. That's what the old lady said. A special cake. And you've got to make him welcome. That's important. You must always keep a special lantern burning out there in the clearing where the deed was done. And you can see, can't you son? We *have* made you welcome. You'll always be our boy. Nothing can change that.'

Stuart banged his fist down hard on the table in anger, making the guttering candles on the cake shake, creating new shadows which leapt threateningly from the corners of the room. The old woman cried out in alarm, and the old man seized him by the wrist.

'Matthew! We've done everything that the gypsy woman said. But I should warn you. Arnold has put pieces of silver into the cartridges of his shotgun. Violet! Cut the cake!'

This is absolutely bloody crazy! thought Stuart. And then the nightmare and its logic suddenly fitted together perfectly. The whole insane sequence of events began to make sense.

Quietly, Stuart leaned across to the old man.

'I'm not Matthew. But he *is* out there - somewhere in the dark. I know he's a werewolf. He attacked me out there on the road and followed me up to the farm. He's come back all right and he's out there prowling around the house. I don't know whether this... this... ritual is supposed to placate him or something. But *believe* me... you've got the wrong person.'

The old woman shoved a plate across the table with a wedge of cake on it. It came to rest with a rattle, right in front of Stuart. Two warped candles flickering madly from the concrete-hard icing.

'Eat!'

'What?' gasped Stuart incredulously. 'You must be joking...' A grey worm, cut in half by the cake knife, writhed and squirmed its way free from the cake mixture onto the plate.

'Eat!'

A gossamer thread of cobweb was caught in the flame of one of the candles and it hissed as it dissolved. With stomach heaving, Stuart picked up the piece of cake and looked at the trio sitting around the table. Sitting there, in their paper hats, the shadows from the candles creeping and fluttering on their faces. For all the world it looked as if they were engaged in some weird grimacing competition.

'Eat!'

The room vibrated to the ululating howl of a savage wolf.

Stuart dropped the cake and leapt backwards in his chair from sheer fright - which probably saved his life. As he fell to the floor, there was an ear shattering roar as the shotgun spat bright yellow flame and sparks across the table and huge slivers of wood were ripped from the wall where Stuart had been sitting. The recoil sent Arnold hurtling backwards.

Hell had suddenly erupted in the cottage.

The fly-blown window beside the oak door suddenly exploded into a thousand glittering fragments, and as Stuart rolled on the floor he had the impression that a long clawed arm had come thrusting through the window.

The old woman screamed again as a howling wind blasted through the gaping aperture and blew out all the candles on the cake. The lantern crashed to the floor and fizzled out. Above the noise of the howling wind, and the reverberating echo of the shotgun blast, Stuart could make out the old man's voice sobbing in the darkness.

'Matthew! Matthew! We *did* love you.'

The large oak door shuddered violently under the massive weight of something outside. Hammering. Scratching. Ripping. The bolt of the door rattled and clattered noisily. With the rending noise of a tree being felled, the hinges on the door screeched in protest as the oak burst inwards. Lying on the floor, Stuart tried to avoid the oak panelling as it crashed to the floor. But a length of wood struck him on the shoulder as he tried to rise, and knocked him to the ground yet again. For an instant, the door frame was blackened by something entering. And then Stuart could see the moon shining brightly in the sky as the figure passed.

Something had come into the room.

And as it passed, Stuart heard a voice. Not a human voice. More like an inhuman snarling from behind a mask. Muzzled. Spoken through lips that were never meant to speak.

Stuart kicked the oak panelling to one side and leapt through the shattered doorway. Trees swam at him crazily as he blundered panic-stricken through the undergrowth, expecting the nightmare padding sound of clawed feet and inhuman panting which would mean that the thing was pursuing him again. Out into the main road again, he never looked back for fear of seeing that abominable shape crashing through the bushes after him.

* * *

Of his flight back into civilisation, he could never really remember very much - and would never have thought it possible that he could run twelve miles back to town. But he did.

In the months to come, the fact that Crowfast Farm didn't appear on any map didn't really surprise him. And when, three years later, he passed that bend in the road again where he had crashed over the gate, he wasn't at all surprised to find that there was no gate in evidence. He didn't even bother to look for the signpost which indicated that Crowfast Farm was two miles up the road. He knew it wouldn't be there.

He would have doubted his sanity if it hadn't been for one thing. The warped birthday candle which he had found in his pocket.

The whole sequence of events would never be very clear again. But the voice which Stuart had heard in the doorway would stay with him forever. Inhuman it may have been. And spoken in a horribly distorted voice. But the words were clear enough.

Matthew had returned home to even the score.

'*Many Happy Returns.*'

MACKINTOSH WILLY

by

Ramsey Campbell

To start with, he wasn't called Mackintosh Willy. I never knew who gave him that name. Was it one of those nicknames that seem to proceed from a group subconscious, names recognized by every member of the group yet apparently originated by none? One has to call one's fears something, if only to gain the illusion of control. Still, sometimes I wonder how much of his monstrousness we created. Wondering helps me not to ponder my responsibility for what happened at the end.

When I was ten I thought his name was written inside the shelter in the park. I saw it only from a distance; I wasn't one of those who made a game of braving the shelter. At ten I wasn't afraid to be timid - that came later, with adolescence.

Yet if you had walked past Newsham Park you might have wondered what there was to fear: why were children advancing, bold but wary, on the red-brick shelter by the twilit pool? Surely there could be no danger in the shallow shed, which might have held a couple of dozen bicycles. By now the fisherman and the model boats would have left the pool alone and still; lamps on the park road would have begun to dangle luminous tails in the water. The only sounds would be the whispering of children, the murmur of trees around the pool, perhaps a savage incomprehensible muttering whose source you would be unable to locate. Only a game, you might reassure yourself.

And of course it was: a game to conquer fear. If you had waited long enough you might have heard shapeless movement in the shelter, and a snarling. You might have glimpsed him as he came scuttling lopsidedly out of the shelter, like an injured spider from its lair. In the gathering darkness, how much of your glimpse would you believe? The unnerving swiftness of the obese limping shape? The head which seemed to belong to another, far smaller, body, and which was almost invisible within a grey Balaclava cap, except for the small eyes which glared through the loose hole?

All of that made us hate him. We were too young for tolerance - and besides, he was intolerant of us. Ever since we could remember he had been there, guarding his territory and his bottle of red biddy. If anyone ventured too close he would start muttering. Sometimes you could hear some of the words: 'Damn bastard prying interfering snooper... thieving bastard layabout... think you're clever, eh? ...I'll give you something clever...'

We never saw him until it was growing dark: that was what made him into a monster. Perhaps during the day he joined his cronies elsewhere - on the steps of ruined churches in the centre of Liverpool, or lying on the grass in St John's Gardens, or crowding the benches opposite Edge Hill Public Library, whose stopped clock no doubt helped their draining of time. But if anything of this occurred to us, we dismissed it as irrelevant. He was a creature of the dark.

Shouldn't this have meant that the first time I saw him in daylight was the end? In fact, it was only the beginning.

It was a blazing day at the height of summer, my tenth. It was too hot to think of games to while away my school holidays. All I could do was walk errands for my parents, grumbling a little.

They owned a small newsagent's on West Derby Road. That day they were expecting promised copies of the *Tuebrook Bugle*. Even when he disagreed with them, my father always supported the independent newspapers - the *Bugle*, the *Liverpool Free Press*: at least they hadn't been swallowed or destroyed by a monopoly. The lateness of the *Bugle* worried him; had the paper given in? He sent me to find out.

I ran across West Derby Road just as the traffic lights at the top of the hill released a flood of cars. Only girls used the pedestrian subway so far as I was concerned; besides, it was flooded again. I strolled past the concrete police station into the park, to take the long way round. It was too hot to go anywhere quickly or even directly.

The park was crowded with games of football, parked prams, sunbathers draped over the greens. Patients sat outside the hospital on Orphan Drive beside the park. Around the lake, fishermen sat by transistor radios and whipped the air with hooks. Beyond the lake, model boats snarled across the shallow circular pool. I stopped to watch their patterns on the water, and caught sight of an object in the shelter.

At first I thought it was an old grey sack that someone had dumped on the bench. perhaps it held rubbish - sticks which gave parts of it an angular look. Then I saw that the sack was an indeterminate stained garment, which might have been a mackintosh or raincoat of some kind. What I had vaguely assumed to be an ancient shopping bag, resting next to the sack, displayed a ragged patch of flesh, and the dull gleam of an eye.

Exposed to daylight, he looked even more dismaying: so huge and still, less stupefied than dormant. The presence of the boatmen with their remote-control boxes reassured me. I ambled past the allotments to Pringle Street, where a terraced house was the editorial office of the *Bugle*.

Our copies were on the way, said Chrissie Maher the editor, and insisted on making me a cup of tea. She seemed a little upset when, having gulped the tea, I hurried out into the sudden rain. Perhaps it was rude of me not to wait until the rain had stopped - but on this parched day I wanted to make the most of it, to bathe my face and bare arms in the onslaught, gasping almost hysterically.

By the time I had passed the allotments, where cabbages rattled like toy machine-guns, the downpour was too heavy even for me. The park provided little cover; the trees let fall their own belated storms, miniature but drenching. The nearest shelter was by the pool, which had been abandoned to its web of ripples. I ran down the slippery tarmac hill, splashing through puddles, trying to blink away rain, hoping there would be room in the shelter.

There was plenty of room, both because the rain reached easily into the depths of the brick shed and because the shelter was not entirely empty. He lay as I had seen him, face upturned within the sodden Balaclava. Had the boatmen avoided looking closely at him? Raindrops struck his unblinking eyes and trickled over the patch of flesh.

I hadn't seen death before. I stood shivering and fascinated in the rain. I needn't be scared of him now. He'd stuffed himself into the grey coat until it split in several places; through the rents I glimpsed what might have been dark cloth or discoloured hairy flesh. Above him, on the shelter, were graffiti which at last I saw were not his name at all, but the names of three boys: MACK TOSH WILLY. They were partly erased, which no doubt was why one's mind tended to fill the gap.

I had to keep glancing at him. He grew more and more difficult to ignore; his presence was intensifying. His shapelessness, the rents in his coat, made me think of an old bag of washing, decayed and mouldy. His hand lurked in his sleeve; beside it, amid a scattering of Coca-Cola caps, lay fragments of the bottle whose contents had perhaps killed him. Rain roared on the dull green roof of the shelter; his staring eyes glistened and dripped. Suddenly I was frightened. I ran blindly home.

'There's someone dead in the park,' I gasped. 'The man who chases everyone.'

'Look at you!' my mother cried. 'Do you want pneumonia? Just you get out of those wet things this instant!'

Eventually I had a chance to repeat my news. By this time the rain had stopped. 'Well, don't be telling us,' my father said. 'Tell the police. They're just across the road.'

Did he think I had exaggerated a drunk into a corpse? He looked surprised when I hurried to the police station. But I couldn't miss the chance to venture in there - I believed that elder brothers of some of my schoolmates had been taken into the station and hadn't come out for years.

Besides a window which might have belonged to a ticket office was a bell which you rang to make the window's partition slide back and display a policeman. He frowned down at me. What was my name? What had I been doing in the park? Who had I been with? When a second head appeared beside him he said reluctantly, 'He thinks someone's passed out in the park.'

A blue-and-white Mini called for me at the police station, like a taxi; on the roof a red sign said POLICE. People glanced in at me as though I were on my way to prison. Perhaps I was: suppose Mackintosh Willy had woken up and gone? How long a sentence did you get for lying? False diamonds sparkled on the grass and in the trees. I wished I'd persuaded my father to tell the police.

As the car halted, I saw the grey bulk in the shelter. The driver strode, stiff with dignity, to peer at it. 'My God,' I heard him say in disgust.

Did he know Mackintosh Willy? Perhaps, but that wasn't the point. 'Look at this,' he said to his colleague. 'Even see a corpse with pennies on his eyes? Just look at this, then. See what someone thought was a joke.'

He looked shocked, sickened. He was blocking my view as he demanded, 'Did you do this?'

His white-faced anger, and my incomprehension, made me speechless. But his colleague said, 'It wouldn't be him. He wouldn't come and tell us afterwards would he?'

As I tried to peer past them he said, 'Go on home, now. Go on.' His gentleness seemed threatening. Suddenly frightened, I ran home through the park.

For a while I avoided the shelter. I had no reason to go near, except on the way home from school. Sometimes I'd used to see schoolmates tormenting Mackintosh Willy; sometimes, at a distance, I had joined them. Now the shelter yawned emptily, baring its dim bench. The dark pool stirred, disturbing the green beards of the stone margin. My main reason for avoiding the park was that there was nobody with whom to go.

Living on a main road was the trouble. I belonged to none of the side streets, where they played football among parked cars or chased through the back alleys. I was never invited to street parties. I felt like an outsider, particularly when I had to pass the groups of teenagers who sat on the railings above the pedestrian subway, lazily swinging their legs, waiting to pounce. I stayed at home, in the flat above the newsagent's, when I could, and read everything in the shop. But I grew frustrated: I did enough reading at school. All this was why I welcomed Mark. He could save me from my isolation.

Not that we became friends immediately. He was my parents' latest paperboy. For several days we examined each other warily. He was taller than me, which was intimidating, but seemed unsure how to arrange his lankiness. Eventually he said, 'What're you reading?'

He sounded as though reading was a waste of time. 'A book.' I retorted.

At last, when I'd let him see it was Mickey Spillane, he said, 'Can I read it after you?'

'It isn't mine. It's the shop's.'

'All right so I'll buy it' He did so at once, paying my father. He was certainly wealthier than me. When my resentment of his gesture had cooled somewhat, I realized that he was letting me finish what was now his book. I dawdled over it to make him complain, but he never did. Perhaps he might be worth knowing.

My instinct was accurate: he proved to be generous - not only with money, though his father made plenty of that in home improvements, but also in introducing me to his friends. Quite soon I had my place in the tribe at the top of the pedestrian subway, though secretly I was glad that we never exchanged more than ritual insults with other gangs. Perhaps the police station, looming in the background, restrained hostilities.

Mark was generous too with his ideas. Although Ben, a burly lad, was nominal leader of the gang, it was Mark who suggested most of our activities. Had he taken to delivering papers to save himself from boredom - or, as I wondered afterwards, to distract himself from his thoughts? It was Mark who brought his skates so that we could brave the slope of the pedestrian subway, who let us ride his bicycle around the side streets, who found ways into derelict houses, who brought his transistor radio so that we could hear the first Beatles records as the traffic passed unheeded on West Derby Road. But was all this a means of distracting us from the park?

No doubt it was inevitable that Ben resented his supremacy. Perhaps he deduced, in his slow and stolid way, that Mark disliked the park. Certainly he hit upon the ideal method to challenge him.

It was a hot summer evening. By then I was thirteen. Dust and fumes drifted in the wakes of cars; wagons clattered repetitively across the railway bridge. We lolled about the pavement, kicking Coca-Cola caps. Suddenly Ben said, 'I know something we can do.'

We trooped after him, dodging an aggressive gang of taxis, towards the police station. He might have meant us to play some trick there; when he swaggered past, I'm sure everyone was relieved - everyone except Mark, for Ben was leading us onto Orphan Drive.

Heat shivered above the tarmac. Beside us in the park, twilight gathered beneath the trees, which stirred stealthily. The island in the lake creaked with ducks; swollen litter drifted sluggishly, or tried to climb the bank. I could sense Mark's nervousness. He had turned his radio louder; a misshapen Elvis Presley blundered out of the static, then sank back into incoherence as a neighbouring wave band seeped into his voice. Why was Mark on edge? I could see only the dimming sky, trees on the far side of the lake diluted by haze, the gleam of bottle caps like eyes atop a floating mound of litter, the glittering of broken bottles in the lawns.

We passed the locked ice-cream kiosk. Ben was heading for the circular pool, whose margin was surrounded by a fluorescent orange tape tied between iron poles, a makeshift fence. I felt Mark's hesitation, as though he were a scared dog dragged by a lead. The lead was pride: he couldn't show fear, especially when none of us knew Ben's plan.

A new concrete path had been laid around the pool. 'We'll write our names in that,' Ben said.

The dark pool swayed, as though trying to douse reflected lights. Black clouds spread over the sky and loomed in the pool; the threat of a storm lurked behind us. The brick shelter was very dim, and looked cavernous. I strode to the orange fence, not wanting to be last, and poked the concrete with my toe. 'We can't,' I said; for some reason I felt relieved. 'It's set.'

Someone had been there before us, before the concrete had hardened. Footprints led from the dark towards us. As they advanced, they faded, no doubt because the concrete had been setting. They looked as though the man had suffered from a limp.

When I pointed them out, Mark flinched, for we heard the radio swing wide of comprehensibility. 'What's up with you?' Ben demanded.

'Nothing.'

'It's getting dark,' I said, not as an answer but to coax everyone back towards the main road. But my remark inspired Ben; contempt grew in his eyes. 'I know what it is,' he said, gesturing at Mark. 'This is where he used to be scared.'

'Who was scared? I wasn't bloody scared.'

'Not much you weren't. You didn't look it,' Ben scoffed, and told us, 'Old Willy used to chase him all round the pool. He used to hate him, did old Willy. Mark used to run away from him. I never. *I* wasn't scared.'

'You watch who you're calling scared. If you'd seen what I did to that old bastard -'

Perhaps the movements around us silenced him. Our surroundings were crowded with dark shifting: the sky unfurled darkness, muddy shapes rushed at us in the pool, a shadow huddled restlessly in one corner of the shelter. But Ben wasn't impressed by the drooping boast. 'Go on,' he sneered. 'You're scared now. Bet you wouldn't dare go in his shelter.'

'Who wouldn't? You watch it, you!'

'Go on, then. Let's watch you do it.'

We must all have been aware of Mark's fear. His whole body was stiff as a puppet's. I was ready to intervene - to say, lying, that the police were near - when he gave a shrug of despair and stepped forward. Climbing gingerly over the tape as though it were electrified, he advanced onto the concrete.

He strode towards the shelter. He had turned the radio full on; I could hear nothing else, only watch the shifting of dim shapes deep in the reflected sky, watch Mark stepping in the footprints for bravado. They swallowed his feet. He was nearly at the shelter when I saw him glance at the radio.

The song had slipped awry again; another wave band seeped in, a blurred muttering. I thought it must be Mark's infectious nervousness which made me hear it forming words. 'Come on, son. Let's have a look at you.' But why shouldn't the words have been real, fragments of a radio play?

Mark was still walking, his gaze held by the radio. He seemed almost hypnotised; otherwise he would surely have flinched back from the huddled shadow which surged forward from the corner by the bench, even though it must have been the shadow of a cloud.

As his foot touched the shelter I called nervously. 'Come on, Mark. Let's go and skate.' I felt as though I'd saved him. But when he came hurrying back, he refused to look at me or at anyone else.

For the next few days he hardly spoke to me. Perhaps he thought of avoiding my parents' shop. Certainly he stayed away from the gang - which turned out to be all to the good, for Ben, robbed of Mark's ideas, could think only of shoplifting. They were soon caught, for they weren't very skilful. After that my father had doubts about Mark, but Mark had always been scrupulously honest in deliveries; after some reflection, my father kept him on. Eventually Mark began to talk to me again, though not about the park.

That was frustrating: I wanted to tell him how the shelter looked now. I still passed it on my way home, though from a different school. Someone had been scrawling on the shelter. That was hardly unusual - graffiti filled the pedestrian subway, and even claimed the ends of streets - but the words were odd, to say the least: like scribbles on the walls of a psychotic's cell, or the gibberish of an invocation. DO THE BASTARD. BOTTLE UP HIS EYES. HOOK THEM OUT. PUSH HIS HEAD IN. Tangled amid them, like chewed bones, gleamed the eroded slashes of MACK TOSH WILLY.

I wasn't as frustrated by the conversational taboo as I might have been, for I'd met my first girl friend. Kim was her name; she lived in a flat on my block, and because of her parents' trade, seemed always to smell of fish and chips. She obviously looked up to me - for one thing, I'd begun to read for pleasure again, which few of her friends could be bothered attempting. She told me her secrets, which was a new experience for me, strange and rather exciting - as was being seen on West Derby Road with a girl on my arm, any girl. I was happy to ignore the jeers of Ben and cronies.

She loved the park. Often we strolled through, scattering charitable crumbs to ducks. Most of all she loved to watch the model yachts, when the snarling model motorboats left them alone to glide over the pool. I enjoyed watching too, while holding her warm, if rather clammy, hand. The breeze carried away her culinary scent. But I couldn't help noticing that the shelter now displayed screaming faces with red bursts for eyes. I have never seen drawings of violence on walls elsewhere.

My relationship with Kim was short-lived. Like most such teenage experiences, our parting was not romantic and poignant, if partings ever are, but harsh and hysterical. It happened one evening as we made our way to the fair which visited Newsham Park each summer.

Across the lake we could hear shrieks that mingled panic and delight as cars on metal poles swung girls into the air, and the blurred roaring of an ancient pop song, like the voice of an enormous radio. On the Ferris wheel, coloured lights sailed up, painting airborne faces. The twilight shone like a Christmas tree; the lights swam in the pool. That was why Kim said, 'Let's sit and look first.'

The only bench was in the shelter. Tangles of letters dripped tails of dried paint, like blood; mutilated faces shrieked soundlessly. Still, I thought I could bear the shelter, Sitting with Kim gave me the chance to touch her breasts, such as they were, through the collapsing deceptively large cups of her bra. Tonight she smelled of newspapers, as though she had been wrapped in them for me to take out; she must have been serving at the counter. Nevertheless I kissed her, and ignored the fact that one corner of the shelter was dark as a spider's crevice.

But she had noticed; I felt her shrink away from the corner. Had she noticed more than I? Or was it her infectious wariness which made the dark beside us look more solid, about to shuffle towards us along the bench? I was uneasy but the din and the lights of the fairground were reassuring. I determined to make the most of Kim's need for protection, but she pushed my hand away. 'Don't,' she said irritably, and made to stand up.

At that moment I heard a blurred voice. 'Popeye,' it muttered as if to itself; it sounded gleeful. 'Popeye.' Was it part of the fair? It might have been a stallholder's voice, distorted by the uproar, for it said, 'I've got something for you.'

The struggles of Kim's hand in mine excited me. 'Let me go,' she was wailing. Because I managed not to be afraid, I was more pleased than dismayed by her fear - and I was eager to let my imagination flourish, for it was better than reading a ghost story. I peered into the dark corner to see what horrors I could imagine.

Then Kim wrenched herself free and ran around the pool. Disappointed and angry, I pursued her. 'Go away,' she cried. 'You're horrible. I never want to speak to you again.' For a while I chased her along the dim paths, but once I began to plead I grew furious with myself. She wasn't worth the embarrassment. I let her go, and returned to the fair, to wander desultorily for a while. When I'd stayed long enough to prevent my parents from wondering why I was home early, I walked home.

I meant to sit in the shelter for a while, to see if anything happened, but someone was already there. I couldn't make out much about him, and didn't like to go closer. He must have been wearing spectacles, for his eyes seemed perfectly circular and gleamed like metal, not like eyes at all.

I quickly forgot that glimpse, for I discovered Kim hadn't been exaggerating: she refused to speak to me. I stalked off to buy fish and chips elsewhere, and decided that I hadn't liked her anyway. My one lingering disappointment, I found glumly, was that I had nobody with whom to go to the fairground. Eventually, when the fair and the school holidays were approaching their end, I said to Mark, 'Shall we go to the fair tonight?'

He hesitated, but didn't seem especially wary. 'All right,' he said with the indifference we were beginning to affect about everything.

At sunset the horizon looked like a furnace, and that was how the park felt. Couples rambled sluggishly along the paths; panting dogs splashed in the lake. Between the trees the lights of the fairground shimmered and twinkled, cheap multicoloured stars. As we passed the pool, I noticed that the air was quivering above the footprints in the concrete, and looked darkened, perhaps by dust. Impulsively I said, 'What did you do to old Willy?'

'Shut up,' I'd never heard Mark so savage or withdrawn. 'I wish I hadn't done it.'

I might have retorted to his rudeness, but instead I let myself be captured by the fairground, by the glade of light amid the balding rutted green. Couples and gangs roamed, harangued a shade half-heartedly by stallholders. Young children hid their faces in pink candy floss. A siren thin as a Christmas party hooter set the Dodgems running. Mark and I rode a tilting bucket above the fuzzy clamour of music, the splashes of glaring light, the cramped crowd. Secretly I felt a little sick, but the ride seemed to help Mark regain his confidence. Shortly, as we were playing a pinball machine with senile flippers, he said, 'Look there's Lorna and what's-her-name.'

It took me a while to be sure where he was pointing: at a tall bosomy girl, who probably looked several years older than she was, and a girl of about my height and age, her small bright face sketched with makeup. By this time I was following him eagerly.

The tall girl was Lorna; her friend's name was Carol. We strolled for a while, picking our way over power cables, and Carol and I began to like each other; her scent was sweet, if rather overpowering. As the fair began to close, Mark easily won trinkets at a shooting gallery and presented them to the girls, which helped us persuade them to meet us on Saturday night. By now Mark never looked towards the shelter - I think not from wariness but because it had ceased to worry him, at least for the moment. I glanced across, and could just distinguish someone pacing unevenly round the pool, as if impatient for a delayed meeting.

If Mark had noticed, would it have made any difference? Not in the long run, I try to believe. But however I rationalise, I know that some of the blame was mine.

We were to meet Lorna and Carol on our side of the park in order to take them to the Carlton cinema, nearby. We arrived late, having taken our time over sprucing ourselves; we didn't want to seem too eager to meet them. Besides the police station, at the entrance to the park, a triangular island of pavement, large enough to contain a spinney of trees, divided the road. The girls were meant to be waiting at the nearest point of the triangle. But the island was deserted except for the caged darkness beneath the trees.

We waited. Shop windows on West Derby Road glared fluorescent green. Behind us trees whispered, creaking. We kept glancing into the park, but the only figure I could distinguish on the dark paths was alone. Eventually, for something to do, we strolled desultorily around the island.

It was I who saw the message first, large letters scrawled on the corner nearest the park. Was it Lorna's or Carol's handwriting? It rather shocked me, for it looked semi-literate. But she must have had to use a stone as a pencil, which couldn't have helped; indeed, some letters had had to be dug out of the moss which coated stretches of the pavement. MARK SEE YOU AT THE SHELTER, the message said.

I felt him withdraw a little. 'Which shelter?' he muttered.

'I expect they mean the one near the kiosk,' I said, to reassure him.

We hurried along Orphan Drive. Above the lamps, patches of foliage shone harshly. Before we reached the pool we crossed the bridge, from which in daylight manna rained down to the ducks, and entered the park. The fair had gone into hibernation; the paths, and the mazes of tree trunks, were silent and very dark. Occasional dim movements made me think that we were passing the girls, but the figure that was wandering a nearby path looked far too bulky.

The shelter was at the edge of the main green, near the football pitch. Beyond the green, tower blocks loomed in glaring auras. Each of the four sides of the shelter was an alcove housing a bench. As we peered into each, jeers or curses challenged us.

'I know where they'll be,' Mark said, 'In the one by the bowling green. That's near where they live.'

But we were closer to the shelter by the pool. Nevertheless I followed him onto the park road. As we turned towards the bowling green I glanced towards the pool, but the street lamps dazzled me. I followed him along a narrow path between hedges to the green, and almost tripped over his ankles as he stopped short. The shelter was empty, alone with its view of the decaying Georgian houses on the far side of the bowling green.

To my surprise and annoyance, he still didn't head for the pool. Instead, we made for the disused bandstand hidden in a ring of bushes. It's only tune now was the clink of broken bricks. I was sure that the girls wouldn't have called it a shelter, and of course it was deserted. Obese dim bushes hemmed us in. 'Come on,' I said, 'or we'll miss them. They must be by the pool.'

'They won't be there,' he said - stupidly, I thought.

Did I realise how nervous he suddenly was? Perhaps, but it only annoyed me. After all, how else could I meet Carol again? I didn't know her address. 'Oh, all right,' I scoffed, 'if you want us to miss them.'

I saw him stiffen. Perhaps my contempt hurt him more than Ben's had; for one thing, he was older. Before I knew what he intended he was striding towards the pool, so rapidly that I would have had to run to keep up with him - which, given the hostility that flared between us, I refused to do. I strolled after him rather disdainfully. That was how I came to glimpse movement in one of the islands of dimness between the lamps of the park road. I glanced towards it and saw, several hundred yards away, the girls.

After a pause they responded to my waving - somewhat timidly, I thought. 'There they are,' I called to Mark. He must have been at the pool by now, but I had difficulty in glimpsing him beyond the glare of the lamps. I was beckoning the girls to hurry when I heard his radio blur into speech.

At first I was reminded of a sailor's parrot. 'Aye, aye,' it was croaking. The distorted voice sounded cracked, uneven, almost too old to speak. 'You know what I mean, son?' it grated triumphantly. 'Aye aye.' I was growing uneasy, for my mind had begun to interpret the words as 'Eye eye' - when suddenly, dreadfully, I realized Mark hadn't brought his radio.

There might be someone in the shelter with a radio. But I was terrified, I wasn't sure why. I ran towards the pool calling, 'Come on,

Mackintosh Willy

Mark, they're here!' The lamps dazzled me; everything swayed with my running - which was why I couldn't be sure what I saw.

I know I saw Mark in the shelter. He stood just within, confronting darkness. Before I could discern whether anyone else was there, Mark staggered out blindly, hands covering his face, and collapsed into the pool.

Did he drag something with him? Certainly by the time I reached the margin of the light he appeared to be tangled in something, and to be struggling feebly. He was drifting, or being dragged, towards the centre of the pool by a half-submerged heap of litter. At the end of the heap nearest Mark's face was a pale ragged patch in which gleamed two round objects - bottle caps? I could see all this because I was standing helpless, screaming at the girls, 'Quick, for Christ's sake! He's drowning!' He was drowning, and I couldn't swim.

'Don't be stupid,' I heard Lorna say. That enraged me so much that I turned from the pool. 'What do you mean?' I cried. 'What do you mean, you stupid bitch?'

'Oh, be like that,' she said haughtily, and refused to say more. But Carol took pity on my hysteria and explained, 'It's only three feet deep. He'll never drown in there.'

I wasn't sure that she knew what she was talking about, but that was no excuse for me not to try to rescue him. When I turned to the pool I gasped miserably, for he had vanished - sunk. I could only wade into the muddy water, which engulfed my legs and closed around my waist like ice, ponderously hindering me.

The floor of the pool was fattened with slimy litter. I slithered, terrified of losing my balance. Intuition urged me to head for the centre of the pool. And it was there I found him, as my sluggish kick collided with his ribs.

When I tried to raise him, I discovered that he was pinned down. I had to grope blindly over him in the chill water, feeling how still he was. Something like a swollen cloth bag, very large, lay over his face. I couldn't bear to touch it again, for its contents felt soft and fat. Instead I seized Mark's ankles and managed at last to drag him free. Then I struggled towards the edge of the pool, heaving him by his shoulders, lifting his head above the water. His weight was dismaying. Eventually the girls waded out to help me.

But we were too late. When we dumped him on the concrete, his face stayed agape with horror; water lay stagnant in his mouth. I could see nothing wrong with his eyes. Carol grew hysterical, and it was Lorna who ran to the hospital, perhaps in order to get away from the sight of him. I only made Carol worse by demanding why they hadn't waited for us at the shelter; I wanted to feel they were to blame. But she denied they had written the message, and grew more hysterical when I asked why they hadn't waited at the island. The question, or the memory, seemed to frighten her.

I never saw her again. The few newspapers that bothered to report Mark's death gave the verdict 'by misadventure.' The police took a dislike to me after I insisted that there might be somebody else in the pool, for the draining revealed nobody. At least, I thought, whatever was there had gone away. Perhaps I could take some credit for that at least.

But perhaps I was too eager for reassurance. The last time I ventured near the shelter was years ago, one winter night on the way home from school. I had caught sight of a gleam in the depths of the shelter. As I went close, nervously watching both the shelter and the pool, I saw two discs glaring at me from the darkness beside the bench. They were Coca-Cola caps, not eyes at all, and it must have been the wind that set the pool slopping and sent the caps scuttling towards me. What frightened me most as I fled through the dark was that I wouldn't be able to see where I was running if, as I desperately wanted to, I put up my hands to protect my eyes.

WRITER'S CRAMP

by

David Riley

The Literary Editor of the *Digest of Horror* swung round lazily on his well-worn swivel chair as the morning's mail was brought in. Cartwright-Hughes looked askance down his long, thin, fastidious nose at the heap of battered manila envelopes that were unceremoniously dumped in front of him by the office boy. Another batch of horrors, he thought languidly, and in more ways than one, no doubt! With a quiet sigh of resignation he picked out one of the slimmer envelopes, sliced it open down one edge with a blunt, bone-handled knife and extracted the enclosed batch of densely-typed sheets of paper. His teeth should twinge every time he received one of these, he thought as he surveyed the closely packed lines of typescript. The half dozen foolscap sheets were almost black with thick, smudgily typed letters. Lesson one for all would-be writers, he sermonized acidly, should be: always, but always type with two spaces at least between each line and just now and then, perhaps once every forty years or so, clean the keys of whatever decrepit, pre-Adamite typewriter was being used. Really he shouldn't have to read something like this. It was appalling. Even the edges of the paper were furred from wear. But, unfortunately - the Literary Editor's eternal bane! - the *Digest of Horror* was short, as usual, of publishable material and something would have to be found soon to fill the remaining eight pages in the March issue, which was due at the printers this week.

Cartwright-Hughes settled back as comfortably as his long spine would allow, propped his feet precariously on the edge of his desk and looked at the title heading of the story: *Paper Doom.* At least the title was reasonably original, he thought, pressing gamefully on. But his expectations quickly began to sink into a welter of unreadable Lovecraftian cliches - *bad* Lovecraftian cliches of the *worst* type. This was impossible! Yet, as his eyes scanned further lines, he had to concede that there was, even so, the germ, the merest germ of an idea in it. In some peculiar way the author's grasp of what he was writing about, clumsy though it may have been, did contain a dim air of authenticity. It was difficult for Cartwright-Hughes, who preferred his stories slick, to see just how this was being put over, yet it was there nevertheless.

Finally he flung the manuscript down onto the desk, surprised at himself for having stolidly ploughed all the way through it. Normally he would not have bothered to read more than a couple of pages of any story which was obviously unusable after the first two paragraphs. Reluctantly, he had to admit that the basic plot was good, but the writing, in almost inverse proportion, was horrifically bad. He pulled out a standard rejection slip from drawer in his desk, clipped it to the manuscript and slid it into the stamped addressed envelope which the author had wisely supplied.

There the tale would have ended had it not been for the equally disappointing input of submissions to the *Digest of Horror* contained in the rest of the morning's mail. By noon, Cartwright-Hughes was exasperated and tired. His eyes ached from deciphering the badly typed piles of manuscripts, some of which were blurred with coffee rings and other, less easily identifiable stains, which made him wonder whether some of the putative authors had had sudden, short-lived fits of good taste before sending their manuscripts to him and temporarily made more appropriate use of them for mopping up the floor.

At 12.30 Sykes, the office manager, strolled in with a list of schedules. '*Digest of Horror* is getting awfully close to its deadline, old man,' he intoned potentiously. He was a bald-headed Yorkshireman whose round spectacles seemed to reflect the light like spherical mirrors in a way which Cartwright-Hughes found mildly disconcerting.

Cartwright-Hughes tapped the pile of rejected manuscripts with his foot. 'Literary merit seems to have escaped our hopefuls for the moment,' he said, 'though I suppose something might turn up in the second post.'

'The Last Post will be more appropriate if it's not ready on time. This isn't the only magazine we've got to get ready for the newstands, you know, old man, nor is it our biggest money-maker these days from all accounts, eh?' This was a rather crude reference, delivered with typical Yorkshire bluntness by Sykes, to a sharp but, in Cartwright-Hughes' opinion, temporary slump in the sales of the *Digest*. 'Market fluctuations,' he had said breezily when tackled about it earlier, though he had felt an undeniable twinge of concern. Cartwright-Hughes yawned. 'If the worst comes to the worst I could always write something myself to fill it out.'

'Just so long as it's ready for Thursday,' Sykes said. 'that's the deadline, the *absolute* deadline. We can't wait any later than that.'

By the end of the next day Cartwright-Hughes had taken to gnawing his thumbnails. Tuesday now, there was only one more day to go in which to get the *Digest* finished. To judge from the dismal calibre of amateurish contributions he had been inundated with for the past few months he had no illusions as to what to expect in tomorrow's post. It was like that poem by Yeats, he thought:

'The best lack all conviction, while the worst
Are full of passionate intensity.'

There was only one thing for it, he thought reluctantly as he gazed gloomily at the secretarial staff in the general office through the dusty windows of his own sanctum sanctorum, and that was to dash something off himself. It would mean having to burn some of the proverbial midnight oils unfortunately, but there did not seem to be any realistic alternative. He could, he supposed, have used an old, out-of-copyright reprint, perhaps something from Poe or Bierce, but the *Digest of Horror* was basically a magazine of contemporary fiction. The larger than normal number of old reprints over the past few months had almost certainly been the main reason for the magazine's drop in sales. The task now was to win back its readership. More reprints wouldn't do that. Far from it!

No, there was no other feasible choice. He would have to write something himself.

But what?

Cartwright-Hughes let his fertile imagination amble back over plots he had come across amongst the dirge of unprintable material submitted to the *Digest* recently. Perhaps there was something amongst these which could be quickly chiselled into some kind of presentable shape, but it was usually the hackneyed plots of the contributions that had them skittering back through the post to their authors with rejection slips tagged to their tails rather than just poor or inferior writing. Imagination and, in particular, originality were the things they mainly lacked. Yet there was one recently which he seemed to remember having been impressed with at the time, though its lamentably bad writing had earned it a well-deserved rejection slip.

Abruptly he reached across his desk for the typewriter, tugged it towards him with a triumphant grunt. *Paper Doom* had had a plot he could use, up-dated with a few amendments and additions. The bare bones of its plot would do nicely for the kind of filler he wanted, though he would have to change its title.

With practised ease Cartwright-Hughes' fingers tapped out the title at the head of a clean sheet of A4 paper; *Hand-pressed*, he'd call it, in reference to the affliction the main protagonist in the story would literally have cursed upon him.

The story, which was reasonably straight forward, concerned a man's revenge against his wife's lover. Here Cartwright-Hughes diverged radically from the original story, but *Digest of Horror*'s most popular items often figured tales of gruesome, matrimonial revenge, sometimes, though not always by any means, involving the supernatural. The emphasis was strictly on *horror* and plenty of blood, digestible or otherwise.

The method of revenge was the only real act of plagiarism involved, although Cartwright-Hughes did not feel guilty of even this. After all, he thought defensively, the original story was unpublishable anywhere.

Sticking to the original theme of *Paper Doom,* the vengeful husband, who is depicted as having an academic knowledge of certain forbidden 'Black Arts', sends an old book on demonology to the unsuspecting seducer. On opening the book the man's attention is drawn to a short phrase on the first page which has been written in what looks like brown ink. The ink, of course, is blood. This is the key which immediately unleashes the terrible nemesis which has been sent to him. The page is not paper at all but some kind of thin, leathery substance disturbingly akin to tanned human skin. No sooner has the man read the inscription to himself than the page suddenly starts coming to 'life', wrenching itself free from the binding of the book and hurling itself at the man's right hand, which it completely envelopes. So tight does it cling to him that it seems more like an undersized leather glove - or as if his own hand had suddenly aged into the claw of an ancient corpse.

The repulsive skin cannot, he discovers to his horror, be removed, nor can it be seen by anyone else, as if it was only there in his own imagination. But the real horror comes when he finds, not only has his hand, in his own eyes at least, been hideously disfigured by the raddled, corpse-like skin, but that whenever he is not in complete control of it his hand can unexpectedly act with an apparent will of its own - a will which it soon becomes clear is determined upon his destruction.

The culmination of the story, aimed unerringly at as gruesome a climax as possible, comes when the unfortunate seducer discovers that the only way in which he can rid himself of the curse is to turn it back on its creator. This, sticking again to the plot of *Paper Doom,* is achieved by the victim reciting backwards the original phrase which brought the page to 'life' and severing his hand from his wrist with one chop of a machete. This drives the demonic skin back onto its creator, whose throat is ripped out in a ghastly welter of blood.

With the final gory paragraphs completed Cartwright-Hughes heaved the typewriter back across the desk with a sigh of contentment - a *tired* sigh of contentment. It was now 12.15 a.m., but at least the *Digest of Horror* could go to press complete. And Sykes would have nothing to grumble about for another month.

To Cartwright-Hughes' satisfaction there were no more hitches in the March issue of the *Digest*. Eventually, as sales figures started to come in, they even showed a slight but significant upwards climb, confirming for him his diagnosis for its recent slump. From now on, God willing, there would be no more reprints from the 'mouldy oldies', as one irate reader had referred to them, but brand new, garish, matrimonial bloodbaths, of the type which the *Digest*'s readership apparently lapped up with enthusiasm - but then Cartwright-Hughes had never had any great respect for the readership of the *Digest of Horror*. As he had once expressed it to a colleague: 'Always presume that your average reader is about twelve years old, spotty, sadistic and partially illiterate, and you can't go far wrong.'

Less than a week later he received a small, buff envelope in the post addressed to him by name. To his surprise he found that it was from the author of *Paper Doom*. Cartwright-Hughes read it silently to himself, his face growing pale. Finally he jerked back in his chair and swore. 'Cheeky bastard!' he exploded indignantly.

'Anything the matter, old man?' Sykes, who had been strolling past the office when Cartwright-Hughes gave vent to his outburst, poked his head through the doorway. Cartwright-Hughes waved the hand-written letter towards him angrily. 'This cheeky son of a bitch is accusing me of stealing his story!'

'And did you?'

Cartwright-Hughes snorted. 'The damn thing was that badly written he couldn't have given it away, never mind have it stolen. The worst I did was to use a couple of his ideas in the last issue of the *Digest*. And ideas aren't copyright, whatever this nut might think to the contrary. He should have felt flattered that I'd used them. At least when I'd finished they were readable, which is more than could be said about the gibberish he wrote.' Cartwright-Hughes reached into his breast pocket for a handkerchief to wipe away the spittle from his lips.

'Write back to him then and put him in his place,' Sykes said. 'If you're right in what you say, he hasn't a leg to stand on.'

Cartwright-Hughes grunted. He had already decided to do this anyway. As Sykes ambled down the general office, shaking his head, Cartwright-Hughes lunged for his typewriter, angry phrases smouldering through his mind. The man had almost threatened him, he thought indignantly. Threatened! He'd see who threatened who. When it came to cutting phrases, there was one thing being an amateur and quite another thing being a professional, and Cartwright-Hughes hadn't got where he was without learning a trick or two.

Cartwright-Hughes glanced at the address on the letter:

A.*J. Dymchurch*, Esq.,
The Laurels, *Watery Lane*,
Oswaldtwistle, *Lancashire*.

Well, Mr Dymchurch, Cartwright-Hughes thought harshly, we'll now see what you're made of. His fingers dived aggressively at the keys on his typewriter, venting his feelings in a machine-gun-like clatter of invective. The cheek of the man had been unbelievable. To demand - to *actually* demand - that he publish an apology in the next issue of the *Digest of Horror* for stealing his story! Cartwright-Hughes growled between clenched teeth. And then, adding insult to injury, to warn him of the consequences if he didn't in vague and bewildering terms like he did! Any psychiatrist, given that letter, would have had the poor fool locked up. Cartwright-Hughes' fingers quickly typed out this point, ending with an explosive exclamation mark which almost broke the key from the typewriter.

'Put this in the first post,' he called out to the office boy as he meandered aimlessly past, throwing the letter, now signed, sealed and addressed, across to him. 'First class post.' That would show that he meant business!

To Cartwright-Hughes' satisfaction the next couple of weeks were spent peacefully on holiday. When he eventually returned to the office, happy, relaxed and suntanned after a much needed break in the Austrian Alps, he found a pile of mail on his desk. 'Good grief,' he muttered as he disdainfully looked over the parcels of manuscripts. He pulled one out. This must contain a novel at the very least, he thought as he weighed its heavy bulk in his hands. It was hardly worth the effort of opening it since the *Digest of Horror*, as everyone should know by now, he thought, never used anything longer than a ten thousand word novelette. Shaking his head Cartwright-Hughes cut the parcel open to see if return postage had been enclosed. To his surprise he found that the parcel didn't contain a typescript at all but a hardbound book. 'What on earth is all this about?' he wondered as he pulled it out.

Clearing the rest of the mail to one side he rested the volume on his desk. It was very old and rather ugly; its wrinkled binding looked as if damp had at one time or another take a firm grip of it and ravaged it with decay. A thick, noxious odour rose mustily from it. After touching it he carefully and fussily wiped his fingers clean on a handkerchief of the clammy feeling the book's cover had coated them with. Something about this disturbed him, but he could not figure out what...or why. Perhaps it was the smell, which was as if some small animal had crawled into the book and died.

Cartwright-Hughes flipped the book open to see if there was anything tucked away inside to indicate who had sent it. It was then, quite suddenly, that warning bells - or their mental equivalent - went off inside his head. He knew instinctively, without any shadow of a doubt, that he must not look at the page facing him, but it was already too late. His eyes were almost compulsively drawn to the dark red letters scrawled across it:

'*Mutato nomine de te fabula narratur.*'

Change the name and the tale is about you? Cartwright-Hughes' fingers briefly touched the jagged writing to smooth the paper, which had begun to wrinkle oddly. As he did so there was a sudden ripple of motion across it and the start of a tear appeared at one end. Cartwright-Hughes jerked his hand from the book in revulsion but the page came with it. Like a tattered, wind-blown moth the parchment flapped about his hand. It was stuck, as if glued to his fingers. Vainly he shook his hand to throw the thing from him, but the wrinkled parchment clung tenaciously to him, enfolding itself about his hand. Cartwright-Hughes knew that this was ridiculous. It was as if he had blundered into that trite story he had had so much trouble about. But stories like that never happened, not in real life! He clutched, frantically, at the page to tear it from him, but as he pulled it was like trying to rip his own skin from his hand. He cried out in pain and fell back, bewildered, against his desk, slipping to the floor where he wrestled with the thing, but it seemed to have him trapped in an iron vice moulded to the exact shape of his hand. And the vice was tightening. Crushed, his fingers were already starting to go numb. No! *Noooo!* He grunted with exertion, but his fingers could do nothing against the hideous, fleshy parchment that had trapped them.

For a moment Cartwright-Hughes, who was not a strong man, felt dizzy and he knew that he was falling into a faint. When he recovered moments later he saw a circle of faces staring down at him.

'Are you all right, old man?' Sykes asked as he pushed a folded jacket beneath his head. 'Take it easy. Don't rush to get up.'

Cartwright-Hughes breathed deeply. He had passed out, that was all, he thought. Overwork probably. A feeling of relief passed over him. It had, after all, been nothing worse than a nightmare as he lay sprawled out on the floor.

Slowly, Sykes helped him to his feet while someone fetched a chair. As he sat down, Cartwright-Hughes glanced at his hands.

'Is anything wrong?' Sykes asked; he gripped Cartwright-Hughes' shoulder to steady him, certain that he was about ready to collapse again. But Cartwright-Hughes rallied himself, though he remained silent for the moment as the full horror of it all started to sink in. He knew that there was no point in saying anything now, not now, because no one, no one but himself, would ever be able to see it. He stared in horrified silence at the wrinkled 'glove' that covered his hand like a membrane of ancient skin.

When he finally felt strong enough to stand up he asked Sykes if he would drive him home. 'Anything to oblige, old man,' Sykes responded with the kind of over-enthusiasm people often adopt towards those they consider invalids. Subduing the irritation he would have normally reacted to this with, Cartwright-Hughes walked with him to the car park. Sykes' amiable if aimless chatter passed him unheard as he pondered on the situation he now found himself in. Every moment or so he glanced at his hand as if hoping that eventually he would find that there was nothing there and that it had all been an hallucination after all, but the wrinkled skin was there every time, and he knew, deep down, that this was no hallucination. It was real. Horribly, horribly real!

* * *

He thought back over the plot of *Paper Doom*. He had no doubts as to the source of the thing that had afflicted him. A.J. Dymchurch, Esq., he was the man. He was the man all right, the dirty, vindictive...! Cartwright-Hughes drew his lips back taut across his teeth in a fit of fury. Yet at the same time a grim chill of foreboding crept through him as he looked back over the story he had partially purloined. As Sykes turned the ignition in the heavy Wolseley saloon and drove them out onto the busy main road, heading towards St. Johns Wood, Cartwright-Hughes wondered whether the rest of the 'curse' as depicted in Dymchurch's story would follow, in particular the determination of his disfigured hand to kill him. He stared distrustfully at it. While he was in conscious control of it he knew he was safe, but how could he possibly keep this up all the time? It was impossible, and he knew it. Yet, would he have to go to the violent extreme depicted in the story to free himself of it? He shuddered nauseously at the thought. A squeamish man at the best of times when faced with reality, he found the whole idea inconceivable.

Sykes left him outside the entrance to the select block of flats in which he lived. As he hurried in, the doorman called out: 'Just one letter today, sir.' Thanking him, Cartwright-Hughes accepted it from him and hastened to the lift. He clutched the small, buff envelope in his left hand, having developed a sudden aversion to using the other 'contaminated' hand for anything, especially this: one glance at the crabbed handwriting on the front of the envelope was enough to inform him of the identity of the sender.

Safely back in his flat, with its broad view of St. Johns Wood, Cartwright-Hughes poured himself a strong gin and tonic and put a record on the music centre, choosing a favourite Mozart concerto to help ease the tension that had gripped him and to restore at least the semblance of some kind of normality. Gripping the gin gratefully he settled back in an armchair by the window and carefully unsealed the letter.

'*Dear Mr Cartwright-Hughes,*' it read, '*You will have by now received the book I sent to you, and taken possession of the page enclosed in it. After the way in which you criminally stole the story I sent to you I doubt whether you are uncertain of what will happen next. You have been warned once already. That should have been enough. Yet I am not a heartless man. There is still time. If you carry out what I set out in my previous letter to you I can reverse what has happened. But time is short. And getting shorter. I must have your reply, in writing, soon or it will be too late. Yours, etc.,* A.J.D.'

Cartwright-Hughes sank back despairingly in the armchair. He knew that he was faced with an insoluble problem. How could he possibly confess publicly to having stolen another writer's story? Not only would that mean his professional ruin but, even more importantly perhaps, it would make him a laughing stock from now on with everyone he knew. It was downright impossible for him to do anything like this. Impossible! He might just as well cut his own throat. There was no way in which he could expose himself like that, whatever the cost.

Abruptly, he jumped to his feet, put away the gin and strode into the study in the next room where he unlocked the writing bureau in which he kept his personal mail and laid out a clean sheet of paper. Drawing up a chair, he started to write out a reply to Dymchurch, a reply that was radically different to the one he had sent to him before. As he wrote he avoided as much as possible looking at the wrinkles and creases of dried skin that covered his hand. Instead he concentrated on trying to write something conciliatory to Dymchurch, something which would enable him to avoid the personal and professional suicide of confessing to plagiarism. Ideas floated through his mind as he wrote. An offer of money - a substantial offer of money - was one. Another was the offer of a series of stories in future issues of the *Digest*, although that was certain to send sales plummeting to an all time record low. Play on his vanity, he thought cynically. That was the thing. If Dymchurch could go to the extremes he had in revenge for taking a couple of ideas from his story the man must have an obsessive ego. He must have!

Cartwright-Hughes paused to trace back over what he had written. As he glanced at the letter his face became deathly pale, and a tremor started to pulse in his lower lip.

'*Don't waste your time pathetically pleading. The terms have been stated. Either accept them or face the consequences. There is no other choice.*'

Cartwright-Hughes stared at the crabbed handwriting bewilderedly. His right hand felt even more alien to him now than before. It wasn't his at all any more. It was possessed, *stolen!*

He picked up a paper knife and gently tried to prise the 'skin' away, but it was no use. The thing wouldn't budge except if he cut his own skin away at the same time. Was that the solution then? Get some back street surgeon to cut the skin, both skins, from his hand? If he did that, though, he might just as well have his hand cut off, since he doubted if so much skin could be replaced through skin grafts. He might be better off, then, having his hand amputated, properly carried out under anaesthetic by a surgeon. At least that way it would be relatively painless. Though he couldn't just go to any ordinary surgeon for a job like that. He'd more likely end up being certified by any reputable doctor. The only kind he could approach. he knew, would be someone who had been struck off, someone crooked.

Fortunately Cartwright-Hughes had his contacts, built up over the years from his habit at one time of sniffing cocaine. Erosion of the nasal passages due to 'snorting' the stuff resulted in the not unusual necessity of having to have plastic surgery performed on his nose. Since cocaine was illegal, he had had to take the prudent step of arranging through a 'friend of a friend' to have the operation performed in a discrete clinic somewhere in Brixton. He remembered the anonymous-looking red-brick tenement where the squall of Reggae all but drowned the screams of untended babies in the surrounding slums. Although he didn't know the 'surgeon's' name, he was told at the time by his contact that the man had once been highly placed in his field until struck off for unethical and somewhat immoral practices.

Cartwright-Hughes thumbed through his personal phone book, then dialled. Half an hour later an appointment had been made for that evening for a large sum of money. He felt sick in the pit of his stomach at what he would have to undergo, but there was no choice. He flexed his fingers. It was almost inconceivable that anything had really changed. It still felt like his own hand. It still felt under his control. But the wrinkled skin sheathing it and the alien writing on the notepaper were clear enough proof that his hand had been possessed. He dared not wait for it to act unexpectedly against him, as he knew it eventually would, to bring about his death. It was like walking about with an assassin attached to the end of his arm.

When, later that day, he ordered a taxi to take him to Brixton for his appointment, Cartwright-Hughes vowed to himself that somehow, in some way he would get his revenge. However clever he might think he was, Dymchurch would not get away with this.

* * *

The diesel train drew up at the station, where it was instantly battered by blasts of rain. Cartwright-Hughes glimpsed a dispiritingly small, untended platform through the dirt-smeared window of the carriage door as he tugged it open. A plain sign read: *Church and Oswaldtwistle*. He shivered as he stepped down onto the platform at the cold, penetrating winds, and clutched his briefcase to him like a shield in his left hand as he hurried to the steps which brought him down to the road. He hurried along till he saw a sign for Union Road. An old man, the flat cap on his head bowed against the rain like a battering ram, was shuffling past. Cartwright-Hughes called out, asking the way to Watery Lane. The old man looked at him with glassy, red-rimmed eyes.

'That'll be up the'er,' he pointed waveringly. 'Tha goes past yon shops o'er there - D'yer see them? You go on past the Co-op, then a sandwich bar, *Scoffs*, then a pub, right on till tha gets to th'end - then tha turns reet. Keep on goin' after that till tha comes t'th'end. Then keep on goin' to tha left.' He rambled on a few more directions which Cartwright-Hughes carefully noted.

'Thank you. Thank you very much,' he said.

'Think nowt on it.'

Cartwright-Hughes thought for a moment, then said: 'I don't suppose you know someone up that way called Dymchurch, do you?'

The old man cocked his head to one side and looked at him shrewdly. 'Albert Dymchurch?'

'It could be. I only know his initials: A.J.'

'Aye, that'll be 'im. Albert Joseph Dymchurch.' He spat eloquently into the gutter. 'If'n I were you I'd steer clear o' that on'. Should 'a' bin locked up years ago.'

'Why?'

'*Why?* 'Cause 'iz brains are addled, that's why. Always 'ave bin.' He grinned confidentially. 'If you're 'ere to certify 'im you'll no' go short o' volunteers to back up what I say. Iz that what you're 'ere for?'

Cartwright-Hughes hesitated, uncertain now whether under the circumstances he had been wise to let anyone know that he was here to see Dymchurch, especially a garrulous old man like this. There were certain to be plenty of questions asked later, and the less anyone knew about him the better.

Noticing his hesitation, the old man chuckled good-naturedly. 'Don't worry yoursen, lad. I'll not press you if'n you don't want to say nothin'. I respects a man 'as'll keep a secret. Too much loose talk these days az it iz. But if'n you are 'ere to lock th'owd blighter up then you've got my blessin's lad. Aye, that you 'ave, all reet.'

Following the old man's directions as the wind and rain gradually died down from being vilely unpleasant to a kind of persistent dreariness, Cartwright-Hughes came some fifteen minutes later to a narrow lane leading between a line of trees. A small terraced cottage faced him there, its neighbours blatantly derelict. Dead ivy covered its stone walls like dried varicose veins. A musty smell of unwashed linen, cats and other domestic animals hung round the door, indication enough of how it would smell inside. There were no curtains at the

THE
LAURELS

windows, only discoloured newspapers held in place by crinkled strips of equally discoloured sellotape. On the unpainted, splintered and damp-swollen door was a small plaque, 'The Laurels' pretentiously painted across it in crumbling 'Olde English' letters.

Cartwright-Hughes rapped officiously on the door and tried to adopt the stance appropriate to a local council official. This, he thought, would give him the best means of gaining entry into the house without rousing any undue suspicions. Brow-beat the bastard first, he thought, with a load of domineering bull-shit - sanitation and hygiene, appropriately enough, were obvious targets he could use. Then...!

There was a muffled creak at the door, quickly followed by another, though neither had any noticeable effect. A further creak followed, impatiently this time, and the door was suddenly tugged open. It jammed just as suddenly on the uneven flagstones inside, leaving a gap just wide enough to squeeze through. The odour of unwashed linen and animals became appreciably stronger and was joined by a further smell of cooking - this appeared to consist mainly of some kind of boiled vegetable, probably cabbage, though Cartwright-Hughes was by no means certain.

'Yes?'

An elderly, narrow-shouldered man in a threadbare cardigan peered round the doorway. His thin, angular, unshaven jaws were clamped tight, tensely, while his pale grey, rather watery eyes scrutinized Cartwright-Hughes through slightly misshapen horn-rimmed spectacles perched at an odd angle on the bridge of his nose. Tiny tufts of greyish hairs sprouted like a kind of sparse, miniaturized sedge from the tip of his nose and the lobes of his reddish ears, accentuating his definitely unkempt appearance.

'Mr Dymchurch?' Cartwright-Hughes enquired, briefcase held tight against his abdomen in bureaucratic fashion. 'Mr Albert Dymchurch?' he added pedantically.

'Ye-es.' Apprehensively Dymchurch glanced at the briefcase much as a downtrodden Roman citizen might have once looked upon the *fasces* of a Senatorial magistrate.

Despite the hatred and anger which had driven him here all the way from London, Cartwright-Hughes realized that he was now beginning to enjoy himself, yes, despite *everything*.

'I've been asked to see you,' he said, 'to check your sanitation. There have been complaints...'

Dymchurch stepped back into the house. ' Please come in, please come in,' he said, ineffectively tugging at the door to widen the gap. 'I shall 'ave to get this fixed some day,' he muttered apologetically as Cartwright-Hughes squeezed through the doorway and followed him into the dim room beyond.

Confusion and dust lay about him in the living room - or whatever Dymchurch chose to term it. An old fashioned sideboard cluttered with books that looked equally old; an open coal fire from which a few sickly looking flames periodically spluttered; several armchairs, of which all but one were covered with piles of still more books; and a 1950's style bicycle propped against one wall, while above the fire place there hung a framed portrait in oils of a thin-faced man with a yellowish complexion and slightly protuberant eyes. The whole room filled Cartwright-Hughes' fastidious soul with revulsion - a revulsion born from the dreary, defeated squalor of it all. Dymchurch stood watching him, his baggy trousers and patched cardigan so in place amongst the upheaval that it almost acted as a kind of camouflage, blending him into the background. Cartwright-Hughes studied this man who had hated him so much as to do what he had done to him. He looked too ineffectual, too old, too decrepit, like a worn-out and senile schoolteacher, to have done all of that.

Dymchurch waited patiently for him to speak.

There was no point now in any further prevarication. Cartwright-Hughes, looking down on Dymchurch from an advantage of an additional six inches, said: 'We've never met before, but you know me. At least, you know me enough to have tried to have me killed.'

Dymchurch's eyes opened wide, apprehensive again and perhaps just a little afraid. His hands fluttered uncertainly to his lips as he spoke, carefully choosing his words. 'You are, I take it, from London - not the council?'

Cartwright-Hughes admitted the obvious. 'Cartwright-Hughes is the name,' he said, unclipping his briefcase. He thumped the heavy book he had been sent onto the floor. Spurts of dust erupted from beneath it, fogging the light from the windows. He reached into his briefcase again and brought out a small package wrapped in oilskins. In carrying out all of these actions he used only his left hand. His right arm was used solely to hold the briefcase pressed to his stomach. Suddenly he let the briefcase drop to the floor and held his arm towards Dymchurch, revealing the stump that terminated at his wrist. The flesh was still covered with gauze from the operation. A dark stain tinged it.

Dymchurch clucked. His eyes peered speculatively at Cartwright-Hughes. He was plainly surprised.

Cartwright-Hughes held the oilskin package to his chest and picked it open. Inside lay a wrinkled hand, *his* hand, his *stolen* hand. He threw it down at Dymchurch's feet.

'You know what will happen next,' he said.

Dymchurch shrugged. 'Whatever will be...,' he murmured. 'I can do nothing to stop you, not now.' He shrugged carelessly. Cartwright-Hughes noticed for the first time a steely glint in the man's otherwise watery eyes. Was that indicative of the harder, tougher part of the man, the part that had given him the will to delve as deeply as he had into whatever realms of forbidden knowledge he had chosen to master?

Cartwright-Hughes straightened his back. 'The tables are turned now, and you can learn what it is like to be cursed. And learn how careless you were to use the same curse against me as you used in your story.' Cartwright-Hughes opened a slip of paper, from which he read: '*Narratur fabula te de nomine mutato!*'

Dymchurch stepped back as the wrinkled skin covering the severed hand started to move. It seemed to heave itself up from the hand, and Cartwright-Hughes could see the red perforations beneath where it had clung, leach-like, to his flesh. Like a deformed moth, the 'skin' flapped itself and rose unsteadily into the air. It was then that Cartwright-Hughes began to suspect that something was wrong. For a start off Dymchurch had developed a tight, little, satisfied smile which threatened momentarily to grow. Why? But worse, he saw that the 'skin' was starting to move, not towards Dymchurch, but towards himself!

Cartwright-Hughes stumbled back, falling over the arm of the chair behind him. The 'skin' suddenly flapped forward. Instinctively he brought the stump of his right hand up to shield his face, but the thing wrapped itself about his wrist for the merest moment, biting into the unhealed wound, before slithering past and flapping towards his face. '*Why?*' Cartwright-Hughes cried out in bewilderment. '*Why?*' The 'skin' slapped hard into his face. Where its abrasive underside touched his flesh it left bright red weals that trickled blood. He clutched at it with his left hand, but the perforations beneath it seemed to burn his fingers as if it was covered with thousands upon thousands of tiny, venomous, razor-sharp mouths that sucked at him. He rolled over as it tightened itself about his throat, as the room began to spin before his eyes and the air seemed to boom inside his ears. 'Why? *Why?*' he choked out, his words all but meaningless as the 'skin' tightened its grip, and blood spurted in hundreds of tiny jets out from beneath it.

Dymchurch strolled curiously over as Cartwright-Hughes collapsed, convulsively choking on the floor. His face was now purple above the livid 'skin' wrapped round his throat, and small, bubbling, mewling sounds were all that escaped from his lips, drawn back agonizingly from his teeth. Dymchurch smiled as the Literary Editor's feet kicked out ineffectually, weakening quickly.

It was fortunate, Dymchurch thought, that he had not stuck to fact all the way through the story he submitted to the *Digest of Horror*, otherwise Cartwright-Hughes would never have tried, without the protection of a pentacle about him, to order a gaunt back to its inhospitable world between the planes. They became terribly, even nastily aggressive about things like that. 'But you should have known,' Dymchurch chided reprovingly to the shuddering remains of Cartwright-Hughes, whose swollen eyes had already started to cloud over, 'that there is the world of difference between fact and fiction, and the two should never be confused. You, of all people, should have known better than that.'

The Authors

Notes on the Contributors

RAMSEY CAMPBELL has been justly described as "perhaps the finest living exponent of the British weird fiction tradition", and in 1991 he was voted the Horror Writer's Horror Writer in the *Observer Magazine*. A lifelong resident of Liverpool and Merseyside, John Ramsey Campbell sold his first story, `The Church in the High Street', to August Derleth in 1962. Leaving school that same year, his first collection, *The Inhabitant of the Lake and less Welcome Tenants* appeared from Derleth's Arkham House imprint two years later. Campbell worked for the Inland Revenue and later in a library until he became a full-time writer and reviewer in 1973. Although his early fiction was heavily influenced by H.P. Lovecraft's Cthulhu Mythos (yet set in a distinctly British milieu), his subsequent books and stories have revealed him to be a unique voice in horror fiction - whether as an anthologist (*Superhorror* aka *The Far Reaches of Fear*, *New Tales of the Cthulhu Mythos*, *New Terrors*, *The Gruesome Book*, *Fine Frights*, *Best New Horror* series, with Stephen Jones), in his collections of short fiction (*Demons By Daylight*, *The Height of the Scream*, *Dark Companions*, *Cold Print*, *Scared Stiff*, *Dark Feasts*, *Waking Nightmares*, *Uncanny Banquet*), or as a novelist (*The Doll Who Ate His Mother*, *To Wake The Dead* (US: *The Parasite*), *The Nameless*, *The Face That Must Die*, *Incarnate*, *Obsession*, *The Hungry Moon*, *The Influence*, *Ancient Images*, *Needing Ghosts*, *Midnight Sun*, *The Count of Eleven*, *The Long Lost*). A multiple winner of both the British Fantasy and World Fantasy Awards, Campbell has also completed several of Robert E. Howard's stories of Solomon Kane, written the novelizations of *The Wolf Man*, *Bride of Frankenstein* and *Dracula's Daughter* under the house name `Carl Dreadstone', and is the author of *Claw* (US: *Night of the Claw*) behind the somewhat obvious alias of `Jay Ramsey'. In 1992 he celebrated thirty years of chilling spines, and the bumper collection of his best short fiction, *Alone With the Horrors*, commemorates the event.

STEPHEN GALLAGHER was born in Salford, Lancashire, and currently lives in the Ribble Valley with his wife and daughter. He graduated with Joint Honours in Drama and English from Hull University in 1975 and worked for a number of British television companies before making his first professional sale as a writer to commercial radio. Gallagher became a full-time freelance writer in 1980, and he went on to script two serials for BBC-TV's popular *Dr, Who* series, *Warrior's Gate* and *Terminus* (which he subsequently novelized under the pseudonym `John Lydecker'), and the BBC's *Moving Targets*. His short fiction has appeared in *The Magazine of Fantasy and Science Fiction*, *Asimov's*, *Ripper!*, *Shadows 9*, *Winter Chills*, *Night Visions 8* and *Fantasy Tales 4*. Early books include *The Last Rose of Summer*, *Dying of Paradise*, *The Ice Belt* and the novelization of the SF movie *Saturn 3*, and among his horror and mystery novels are *Chimera* (which was produced as a television mini-series), *Follower*, *Valley of Lights*, *Oktober*, *Down River*, *Rain*, *The Boat House* and *Nightmare, with Angel*. His latest novel is to be called *Red, Red Robin*.

GRAEME HURRY was born in Dumfries, Scotland but has lived in Preston for many years. He is editor of the Preston SF Group newsletter, and was editor of Bryan Talbot's *Frank Fazakerly* comic. He also co-ordinates the non-book reviews for the British Fantasy Society Newsletter.

STEPHEN LAWS lives in Newcastle upon Tyne, and used to work as a Committee Administrator in local government, before becoming a full time writer in 1992. He has been writing since he was eight, and while at school became a great fan of Horror Films and actor Peter Cushing. During this time he became `Playground Storyteller', giving blow-by-blow renditions of the plots from the horror films he'd sneaked underage into cinemas to see. Bitten by the storytelling bug, he was writing television plays at age 27 and his short stories of the supernatural were published locally and on radio. After winning a fiction competition in 1981, Laws decided to attempt his first novel. The result was *Ghost Train*, published in 1985 to enthusiastic reviews and with a publicity campaign which was banned from railway stations around the country by British Rail, who were concerned that it might alarm their passengers. This initial success has led to further novels such as *Spectre*, *The Wyrm*, *The Frighteners*, *Darkfall* and *Gideon*.

MARTIN McKENNA lives in Rishton, Lancashire. He started getting his illustrations published at the age of 16, early work including *Return to Arkham* with Brian Lumley in Dagon. Since then he has appeared in publications such as *Warlock*, *White Dwarf*, *Interzone* (for which he was voted best illustrator two years running) and others. He also produced a great deal of work for many Games Workshop publications, such as the books *Drachanfels*, *Zaragoz*, *Wolf Riders* and *Ignorant Armies*. He has illustrated a variety of books including *Daggers of Darkness*, *Vault of the Vampire* and *Curse of the Vampire*, *Dead of Night*, *Legend of the Shadow Warriors*, *Moonrunner*, *Return to Firetop Mountain*, *Legend of Zagor*, the *Fantasy Tales* series, *The Giant Book of Fantasy and the Supernatural*, *Shadows Over Innsmouth*, *The Mammoth Book of Vampires*, *The Mammoth Book of Zombies*, *The Mammoth book of Werewolves*, *The Mammoth Book of Frankenstein*, and *Voyages into Darkness*. Also a variety of board games, role-playing games and trading cards.

JIM PITTS lives in Blackburn and is a popular artist whose atmospheric illustrations have graced publications on both sides of the Atlantic. His first sale was in 1971 (David Sutton's *H.P.L. Bibliotheca*) and since then has contributed regularly to *Fantasy Tales*, *Ghosts and Scholars*, *Whispers*, *Weirdbook* and various British Fantasy Society publications. An edition of Catherine Storr's classic *Marienne Dreams* sported an inspired Pitts cover. Jim won the Ken McIntyre award for best amateur artist, and in 1992 and again in 1993 he won the BFS award for best artist.

DAVID RILEY lives in Oswaldtwistle, Accrington. He had his first professional sale at the age of eighteen with 'The Lurkers In The Abyss' in the *Eleventh Pan Book Of Horror Stories*. Since then he has had stories published, both in Britain and the United States, in anthologies by Sphere Books, Doubleday, Robinson Books, Carrroll and Graf, DAW Books and Corgi as well as in magazines such as *World Of Horror, Fear, Fantasy Tales, Whispers*, and *Aboriginal Science Fiction*. Recent anthologies include Stephen Jones' *Mammoth Book Of Zombies*, in which he had a novelette called 'Out Of Corruption', and a Science Fiction story called 'Help-Plants' in *Aboriginal Science Fiction*. He has recently completed a fantasy novel called *Goblin Mire*.

BRYAN TALBOT was born in Wigan and currently lives in Preston. He is the creator of *The Adventures of Luther Arkwright*, the ground breaking alternative world comic strip which started in underground magazines and finished as a triple set graphic novel. Bryan has drawn *Judge Dredd* and *Nemesis* for 2000AD as well as *Batman* and *Sandman* for DC among others. He has just finished his latest graphic work, *The Tale of One Bad Rat*, a contemporary Beatrix Potter story.